BOOK 1 OF THE

RED NIGHT

Xavier's Delight

KITTY KING

For information contact:

http://authorkittyking.com

Cover Design by Gemini Cover Designs

Editing by Susan Keillor and Roxanna Coumans

ASIN: B0BY7N3NQH (eBook)

ISBN : 979-8-9880503-0-8 (Paperback)

First Edition: January 2023

10 9 8 7 6 5 4 3 2 1

Author's Note

This is an extremely dark *erotic* book (meaning it was written *for* the spice scenes) and it should not be your first venture into dark erotica. The villain gets the girl. If you are not okay with that or need a traditional happy ending **this book is not for you**.

All content warnings are listed on my website.

Due to the graphic nature of the sex scenes and most certainly the mental content, would recommend for readers 18 and older.

Chapter One

AN INVITATION

"He said my last set was '*mimicked copies of real work*' and '*filled with emotional naivety.*'" I mocked my advisor's voice.

James and I had been eating lunch on the dry grass in the quad. The wind smelled like autumn was well on its way, making me dread my upcoming classes. I would have to enjoy the break before the stresses of university sabotaged my peace.

"Fuck 'em. You're a great photographer, baby." James leaned over to peck my cheek while attempting to throw his empty paper bag in the recycling bin nearby. He missed, but a pledge from his fraternity caught it and put it in for him.

"Hey, James!" James saluted the underclassman. "Hey, James' girlfriend!" I smiled in reply as he wandered away.

Snagging James' jeans to get his attention, I continued, "I can't ignore his critiques. He's *the* Mr. Devon Hall." My voice was whiny. "I'm supposed to be baking him cupcakes and licking the crumbs off his hairy chest or something. At least, that's what Selyne told me last year. He's already called me into his office this week for more roasting."

Over the last year, Mr. Hall often requested I visit his office hours, sighing with the heavy burden of having me as a mentee. I wasn't great at art, but I tried my best. When I would bring that up, Mr. Hall suggested I visit his studio to watch him work. The way he sometimes looked at me had so far prevented my acceptance.

James was checking social media on his phone, hearting pictures with a blaze of his thumb. He murmured, "Ignore him; keep being yourself. You have talent." He paused on a photo of his friend Mack Donaldson with his new boyfriend. James unliked the image.

Just don't give a fuck was James' philosophy. He could afford that privilege. After his undergraduate, he'd move to California, attend a fancy law school, and make partner at his father's firm. He never had to worry about what he would do for money once he graduated.

I wasted time and my parents' money on an art degree. My father insisted I go to college while he would cover my costs. Art was the only thing I could think of to study. Dad warned me I would never make any money, but he was still supportive when I chose the major. The closer I got to graduation, the more my stomach knotted. I had no plan for what to do after. Maybe I could get a job at a ritzy coffee shop and become independent before the age of thirty-five. Or sell nude photos online before I lost my body.

Rubbing the back of my neck, I glanced around the lawn at the groups of Northview University students lulling about in the sun. The buildings cast nebulous silhouettes on our side of the quad. I envisioned a series of architectural photos for next week's project. While studying the prisms from a nearby stained glass, I was drawn to a tall, dark figure that emerged from the business building.

Xavier Cardell had model looks with sleek black hair perfectly tousled in a way that made it seem as if some girl had just run her fingers through it–which she probably had–and a body that screamed "gym bro." Heir to Cardell Enterprises, the business that owned the majority of town and most everyone in it, he was untouchable. By the way he carried himself, he knew it.

Strolling up to James with a red envelope in his hand, the god himself approached with two leggy blondes by his side. Each woman grasped a muscular, tattooed bicep and appeared discontented, having to walk the same path as the peasants.

"James Stevenson." Xavier's sculpted body stood over my boyfriend, casting a shadow on our little picnic. His darkness caused such an eclipse that I wondered if anyone's light could shine through the void.

James tried not to cough on his dill pickle and replied, "Uh, yeah. That's me. Can I help you?" When he investigated the handsome face, James' jaw fell open slightly. Xavier's face held a chiseled jaw that looked like he was constantly sucking on something bitter. The blondes looked around for someone better to talk to.

"Yeah, I've seen you around." Xavier dropped the

red envelope in James' hand. "Hope you can join us. Oh, and make sure to bring your girlfriend."

Xavier nodded the top of his head toward me, and my skin tingled as if he had just shot a bolt of lightning in my direction. He slowly turned his icy blue eyes to stare at me intensely. I stopped breathing. As if he could tell the effect he had on my body, a corner of his lips lifted ever so slightly before he drifted away with his girls in tow.

I eyed James and the envelope, my heart beating again. He tore into it as I asked, "What is that?"

James pulled out a note of heavy cardstock. He read it carefully, held it out for me, and said in a hushed tone, "It's a Red Night invite. You know, the party I told you about." His eyes wide, he turned to watch Xavier sauntering away.

The party wasn't just any party, and it wasn't just any fraternity. It was "Red Night" at Theta Rho Zeta. TRZ was less of a college brotherhood and more like a secret rich boy underground club entrenched in debauchery. Apparently, if you wanted a wild sex party on the down low, Theta Rho was the place to go.

Getting an invite to their quarterly Red Night was unheard of if you didn't know someone. Not even a "knows someone who knows someone." Students were handpicked for the event by an officer. We had just been invited by the president of TRZ himself. Only the most attractive or those willing to submit themselves to depraved scenarios would earn a coveted spot, or so James told me once in private.

The calligraphy on the invitation listed a date one

month away to be held at the Theta Rho Zeta manor. Instructions indicated that attendees should wear a masquerade mask, if so desired, and present a clean bill of health with their invitation. You were to bring guests only if explicitly stated. Cameras and phones prohibited. Condoms and sex toys provided. There was some legal warning that by attending, you were not to speak of the events.

The bottom of the invite ominously stated:

By attending Red Night, you consent to viewing and participating in any sexual activities that may occur.

James whipped his head back to me. "Oh my god, Marissa." He grinned so widely that his dimples creased his cheeks. "We *are* doing this, right? This could be it for me—us. If you don't want to, it's okay; I'll just—"

"I'm on board; let's go. You've wanted this for so long. I'll enjoy watching you have so much fun... and I've wanted to try this, too." I tried to make my voice sound as excited as my boyfriend's.

Truth was, I was scared. Since we started dating, James shared his sexual fantasies with me, feeling more open than he ever had with anyone, he'd said. He accepted his bisexual identity through our chats. I supported him and agreed to be there while he explored himself more thoroughly.

James gave his friend, Mack, a blowjob once at their fraternity party after they made out for an hour. I was turned on by the whole thing but didn't participate, just watched while James kept his hand in mine. After my twenty-first birthday in the spring, James escorted me to a sex club and gave blow jobs to two men at the same time. I just stood there like a voyeur missing a prominent appendage.

"Awesome! I've heard it gets *crazy*. We'll have an amazing time, I know it." James grabbed my hand on my bag and squeezed it. "I love you."

Dropping my hand, he scanned the area, narrowing his eyes at various couples. No one else was holding a red envelope. James was eager to get me involved in his activities, but I wasn't exactly sure how or *if* I fit into his new life. By agreeing to attend, he likely thought I would earn my orgy participation patch for my Sex Scouts sash.

The following week was the Stevenson's annual Labor Day party. Anytime we had to attend events at the white brick contemporary mansion, I wished time would fast-forward like I was a Sims character. I'd used up the "I have a migraine" excuse, so I was dressed in a peri-winkle wrap dress with a full skirt patterned with daisies. I tucked my long, dark hair under a sunhat.

James picked me up in his Mustang, wearing a tan linen suit. "Hey, babe!" He threaded his fingers through mine and placed them on his lap. "Ready?"

"My head is starting to hurt."

James pursed his lips. "Marissa…"

"All right. Fine. Let's go before I jump out of the car."

His muscle car roared as we took off to the palace of pomposity. "Did you get your test results already?" Over the last week, Red Night was all James talked about.

"Yeah. I did."

"Cool, cool. I got mine back, too." He put the car in fifth gear. "All clean."

"Good. Me, too."

James was silent for a while before saying, "I know Mack isn't coming. I asked."

"Oh. D-did you want him to be there?"

"No." James turned on a classic rock station.

The night he and Mack hooked up, James wanted to get fucked in the ass, but Mack wasn't down with it and ghosted James after their make-out session when he asked. I told James I would peg him if he wanted. We tried a few times, but he told me he wanted the thrill of a real penis.

I didn't know what James had in mind for me to do on Red Night. His sole focus was taking it in the ass. Mine was on not losing my boyfriend. For a while, I considered I wasn't enough for him anymore. Maybe he needed a man. I was unsure how long I could continue to share him as I had been doing.

"Hey, remember The Barge?" James pointed out an outdoor venue near the river. "I think about that night every time I drive past."

I smiled. "Me, too."

Freshman year, my roisterous roommate Elle and I

were at the bar watching a local band when James bopped his way over. Elle introduced us. I didn't think I'd have a shot with a man as attractive as James, but he spent the evening making me laugh, dancing, then kissing me. We fucked in the back of his Mustang after the show. It was the first orgasm I hadn't given myself.

After that night, James and I would see each other around campus at various festivities. He was so charismatic that no one could resist his gravitational pull. Everyone knew him or knew of him. We hooked up at every party until we decided we were "together." I was then known as "James' girlfriend" around the Nighthawk's campus; I didn't even think people knew who Marissa Matlock was.

"We're here!" His voice faked a creepy doom, and he crawled fingers up my arm. James pulled into the wide circular driveway. My armpits became soaked with sweat.

James opened my door for me, and we shuffled across the drive. A butler greeted us at the front entry, and murmurs of conversations filtered through the back windows. Most people were near the sparkling pool in the backyard. James grabbed my hand; I held him tightly. Usually, the parties consisted of stuffy lawyers, but the Labor Day party also included James' snooty aunts and uncles. I was hoping not to get stuck with any of them.

Mr. and Mrs. Stevenson stood near the backdoor, greeting guests as they arrived. Neither made eye contact with me as their pride and joy approached.

James' mother reached out to kiss him on both cheeks, and his father shook his hand.

"Son! Glad you made it." His father's eyes scanned over my head. "Hello, Melinda."

"Dad, it's *Marissa*. You know that." James dropped his father's hand. "We've been together for two years."

"Oh, there's Owen Norton. Excuse me." Mr. Stevenson went to greet his more important visitor.

"*Darling*, I have a few people here I want to introduce you to." Mrs. Stevenson grabbed James' arm from me and led him towards the crowd. I trailed behind them, trying to stay caught up. When we got separated, I decided to grab some champagne to dull the pain in my neck.

By the time I found a circulating waiter and downed two glasses, I had completely lost James. I needed the restroom. I remembered one on the first floor near the family kitchen. Yes, they had more than one kitchen. Before I entered, I paused at James' voice coming from his father's office.

"I don't care, Mother."

"But we can find you someone much more *appropriate*," his mother said.

"Son, I know she's lovely to look at, but you must be careful with those of a lower class."

"It's not like they're destitute. Marissa's dad's a cardiologist, for fuck's sake." Footsteps shuffled to the door. "I'm with Marissa. Get used to it."

When James emerged, I shrunk against the wall. "Oh, hey, babe! You ready to go?" His tanned cheeks were red.

"Yes." James grabbed my hand and led me back to his car.

"I guess you heard that," he said as he drove back to my apartment.

"Yeah, it's not the first time." I recalled his father's lecture about making sure he always wore a condom when he was with me.

"Fuck 'em. That's what I say." He grinned and kissed our interlaced hands. I wished I could be as flippant as James was. His parents' disapproval weighed on me. We wouldn't have a future together. He would leave next year, and I would stay in Northview.

James sat in the driver's seat without moving when we reached my apartment. I sat forward on my seat with my hand on the door. "You're not coming up?"

"Nah, I'm going to the Delta party tonight."

"Oh."

James ducked his head and frowned. "I would invite you, but I know you hate those things."

I nodded. He used to invite me everywhere. But he was right. I would much rather spend a night in with my roomie Sharice. Hopefully, Elle wouldn't barge in and demand we all go out. "Okay. I think there's a new Masterpiece Mystery on anyway."

"I'll send you a text to let you know I made it home safely, but keep your window open."

James would crawl into my bed through my room's balcony via the fire escape on most Friday or Saturday nights, drunk, high, or still rolling on Molly. I would wake up with his face between my legs until I couldn't stand it, needing his dick inside.

"Okay."

"Love you, babe." James leaned over and lightly touched his lips to mine. As I climbed the stairs to my apartment, I hoped one of the girls would be home for entertainment. Sharice was on the sofa when I walked in, playing with her phone.

"Masterpiece Mystery night?" I asked.

"Definitely! Starts in twenty minutes." We watched the show, ate popcorn, and gossiped about her love life. It was my kind of Saturday night.

Later that evening, I snuggled comfortably in my apartment bed. James sneaked through the fire escape and fucked me awake. After he ditched his condom and jumped back into bed, he kissed me and asked, "Babe, you're on board, right? You look weird whenever I mention Red Night."

"I look weird? I don't look weird!" I turned enough to punch his arm.

James laughed and nuzzled me. "I didn't mean weird; you're beautiful. I feel like there's something you're not telling me... you know how you do."

I felt obligated to confess my reservations at some point, and post-coital seemed the best time. Rolling over to face him. I said, "Red Night... Uh... what do you think I should do while you, um. What do you want me to do? In your fantasy, I mean, when we're there. Where do I fit in?" I asked him, trying not to seem desperately insecure.

James was extremely attractive with his dirty blonde hair and pretty boy face, complete with dimples. He got hit on a lot. I was sure I had snagged someone out of

11

my league. He told me to be more secure. He loved me, and there was nothing to worry about. But I couldn't help it, especially now that he seemed interested in having sex with other men more than with me.

"Well, I thought we could play around like we normally do, but with strangers in the room, ya know. I don't even know who's going to be there…" His eyes gleamed. "If Jackson Riley shows up… *damn.* Yeah, I'd love him to just take me. You'd be cool with that, right, babe? I mean, he could fuck me, and you could suck me or continue riding me, or maybe I'd suck him while fucking you… I don't know. We can play it by ear."

I pictured these scenes. James was attracted to the TRZ member and university football player; he noticed Jackson about a year ago. Jackson was gay, so I was unsure how he would feel about "James' girlfriend" tagging along if the two of them ended up having sex at the party. I worried my vagina might scare away James' chances of anal bliss.

"Yeah, that's cool. I don't think I'd feel comfortable having sex with someone else by myself, though. I mean, if it were double penetration, I'm down. We're both cool with that?"

"Yes, baby, I'm definitely cool with DP'ing you with some hot dude there. Maybe eat his cum out of your pussy after." He lifted his eyebrows suggestively while pulling me closer.

I questioned his plan. "So, you'd take my ass then, I mean fully? You'd be okay with someone else in my pussy?" James had never breached my back hole. He used a butt plug to get me used to the sensation but was always more interested in using it on himself.

"Yeah, we can do that… if you want. I mean, babe, honestly, I figured I would be going down on a couple of dudes and then get fucked in the ass while you rode my cock. That's my fantasy, baby. I want to come in your pussy while taking it in the ass." His voice became quieter, "Is that all right with you?" He wet his lip and gently rubbed my arm.

"Yes. Of course." I wanted to make James' fantasy come true. Did I have any fantasies of my own? I wasn't sure. Delving into my own desires felt selfish; he was dealing with sexual identity issues. We ended up focusing more on his journey than mine, but maybe I would figure out what I craved in the process.

Before James, I was inexperienced. I lost my virginity in ten seconds to my high school sweetheart. He and I had sloppy sex after school dances and once under the bleachers during a football game. My first boyfriend at university tied me up with silk ties once, but whenever I'd ask Trevor about his fantasies, he'd say something like, "Just you and fucking your pussy all night long, precious." It wasn't good sex; I never came and sneaked away after to get myself off with my vibrator.

It was difficult, but James made sure I had an orgasm most of the time – only while in cowgirl position and only if he sucked my nipples. I wondered, though, if there was something I was missing. James was always so animated when talking about giving blowjobs or a new position for him and me with some other guy to try.

I hadn't been that passionate about anything, possibly ever.

After discussing his fantasies about what would happen on Red Night, the two of us set up some rules.

I would stick by James. He and I would be together like normal, but with other people around. If some guy decided to join us, we'd both encourage it. James would let them know he was available for butt stuff, and I would fuck or suck James while that happened. Somewhere in there, I hoped to get off, too.

Chapter Two

RED NIGHT

R ed Night had arrived. Waiting for James to pick me up, I paced and triple-checked my purse for essentials: wallet, breath mints, wet wipes, mirror, lipstick, the results of my sexually transmitted diseases test (clean), and birth control pills; no phone because they weren't allowed.

I wore a strapless leather minidress ruched on one side that accentuated my curves, tall leather thigh boots, and no underwear or bra. Those would be unnecessary. I chose a lacy black kitten mask and finished the look with deep red lipstick. My dark hair looked sleek, parted down the middle, stick straight.

"Damn, girl. Where are you off to?" Kinsley, my third roommate, eyed me from our denim blue sofa. I teetered out from my bedroom to grab some water for my parched tongue.

"Oh, um. To a party with James." We weren't supposed to discuss the evening with outsiders.

"Sex club party, huh? Make sure he wraps it up. Have fun!"

James texted that he had arrived. I hurried downstairs and fell into the passenger seat of his classic black Mustang. He looked good in his vintage band tee beneath a corduroy blazer with dark jeans. Blonde hair was spiked to perfection, and his body smelled of the ocean. A black mask was looped around the gear shift. He leaned over to take my hand and kiss my knuckles as I settled in the car. "You ready for this? If you want to back out...."

"No, I want to do this. Yes, I almost threw up three times, but I'm ready now." My hand squeezed his. "Don't worry; I have mints." I stuck out my tongue and waggled it back and forth so he could see the white candy.

James chuckled. "I love you, Marissa." His hazel eyes gazed softly at me before he faced the road and headed off. We were doing this.

As we pulled up to Theta Rho Zeta's compound, a guard met us at a gate station. The butterflies in my stomach fluttered wildly. I hadn't realized how intimidating the place would be. After showing our invitations and licenses, the large wrought iron security gate swung open.

We drove down a straight cobbled lane lit on either side with red glowing lanterns. Just beyond the tree line, guest cottages, tennis courts, and stables were occasionally visible by the dying light of the darkening sky.

Reaching the end of the drive, the Gothic Tudor loomed in front of us. Several chimney spires peaked above the shingled roofs, with their shadows crawling over the driveway. James steered around a three-tiered sparkling fountain to a group of valet drivers (fraternity pledges?) dressed in red coats. He jumped out and tossed his keys to one of the young men. I squeezed myself from the safety of the car, keeping my thighs together, and tried not to lose my balance.

The covered entry of the house boasted several red brick archways. Underneath the largest stood a genuine butler in a tailed tuxedo as well as security staff in yellow T-shirts. A few people were queued near the front door, awaiting entry. I craned my neck to capture numerous leaded glass windows sitting high above us, each glowing with what appeared to be red candlelight. Some contained shadows of people moving within them... already in the throes of lovemaking.

To lessen my anxiety, I told myself that if I couldn't handle this, I would stand back and watch my boyfriend take it up the ass. I would be supportive (*"Go, James! You take that dick!"*) but would disappear to a dark corner of the room and wait.

The waiter approaching with a tray of champagne was a welcomed sight. Reaching for a glass, I downed the bubbles before setting the crystal stem back on the tray while we approached the security team. One man demanded to see our papers and IDs again. I dug mine out of my purse. He inspected my driver's license, then tapped on his computer tablet.

"Marissa Matlock?" He slipped his phone out of his pocket, giving me a suspicious glance. I was the first person he spoke to in line.

"Yep, that's me."

The guard turned his head slightly to talk into his phone and mumbled something like, "Candies on the brink, sir." Then he paused while checking me over, eyeing my dress. "Uh, black." He ended the call and pointed to the next security officer in line.

The next neon yellow shirted man patted me down roughly by groping my curves. He snatched my purse, opened it, and shuffled through its contents, pulling out my birth control pills. Holding the pack up to the light, he considered them a moment.

I shuffled my feet. "Just don't want to get knocked up at an orgy," I said with a wincing smile.

He dropped them back in without a glance at me and handed my bag back, pointing to the open front door. I guess I inadvertently agreed to be manhandled by even presenting myself here.

I paused to wait for my boyfriend to make it past the groper. The security guard felt up James' crotch carefully while looking anywhere but his face. After the fondling, James rolled his eyes as if to say, "Get a load of this guy," and placed my hand on his bent arm as we walked through the front door.

The entryway of the manor was smaller than I would have imagined but boasted dark wooden wainscoting that reached above my height of 5'8". Wide wooden arches opened to various rooms around the entire first level of the house. Veined marble tiled the floor, and a golden chandelier hung steadily above us. An L-shaped staircase was tucked into the left of the entrance. Paned glass doors filled the back of the foyer leading out to an awaiting pool lit with red lights.

Couples, throuples, or groups of students were in the water making out. A woman was sucking off several men in a circular hot tub attached to the pool. Laughter and bass bumps trickled through the open doors. Outside, most people were naked or in skimpy bathing suits.

"Ready?" James led us to our right, which opened to a reception area. The room was crowded with people loudly talking or flirting. Everyone wore such vastly different outfits. Some women wore lingerie with masks, others donned skimpy dresses like me, and still, others were in full costumes or leather bondage outfits. Men were casually dressed for a college party, in business suits, or full-out tuxedos. One man was naked; his average-sized chub hung between his legs as he cozied up to a couple of ladies near the fireplace that took up the far wall.

"Do you recognize anyone?" I asked James. He shook his head. With the masks on, it was near impossible. Most guests wore them, except for those in the pool area. James scanned the room. I clutched his arm and scooted closer to him.

"Should we get a drink first?" he asked.

A large and intimidating presence approached us from behind. A deep voice said, "Glad you could make it. The real party's in my room. Follow me."

James and I turned to face Xavier Cardell, who was slowly walking backward with a smirk. He beckoned us with a finger before spinning on his expensive Italian leather shoes, heading back to the entry. He wore a perfectly tailored black dress shirt and gray pants, no tie or mask. My pussy pulsed at the sight of him.

James put his hand over mine and followed up the stairs. I couldn't exactly make out his eyes through his bandit-style mask, but could feel the excitement buzzing through his body like when he would come over after popping Molly. This was the kind of event James Stevenson lived for.

After tailing a stoic Xavier through several turns, we reached dark wood double doors at the end of a long hallway. "Here we are." Xavier opened both at once, seemingly for dramatic effect.

A large bedroom stood before us, bathed in red candlelight. To the left was a seating area in front of a stone fireplace. A study sat to the right with an oversized desk and tall bookcases. In the far corner, an open door revealed a bathroom. The center of the room was filled with a massive four-poster canopied bed. Red velvet curtains had been tied back to reveal the oversize mattress.

The room was grand in its furnishings, but the activity within made me blush. On the sofa in the seating area were the two blonde women I had seen with Xavier the day he gave James the invitation. The woman on the floor was kneeling to eat the other's cunt as the blonde on the sofa threw her head back with pleasure. A man in a leather mask and nothing else swatted the kneeling girl with a black riding crop hard enough that she was screaming into her friend's pussy.

Two men were on one of the armchairs, one riding

the other's cock while the man sitting (Wait, was that Jackson Riley?) scrunched his face in ecstasy, staring up at his partner with lust hazing his eyes. From my periphery, I saw my boyfriend notice Jackson at the same time as I. James' hand moved from mine down to his crotch, readjusting himself.

There were couples fucking against the wall, on the bed, on the floor, in the window seat, three women pleasuring each other on the desk, and large men walking about stroking themselves, looking for the next hole to stick their dicks into. Each table had a bowl of condoms displayed like candy. The grunts, moans, and screams instantly made me damp between my legs, and the room was filled with the smell of latex and cum.

Xavier turned to look at us, well, at James. "Have fun," he said with a sly grin, then ambled off and took a position in a wingback armchair near the fireplace, monitoring the festivities. A beautiful redheaded woman dressed in leopard print lingerie slinked closer and kneeled between his legs. She placed her cheek on his open thigh and said something to him. He lowered his head towards her for a moment, then looked away as if she didn't exist.

James removed his mask and jacket, tossing both onto an empty chair next to the door. Most people here were naked and maskless. I recognized some faces from parties around campus, but I didn't know anyone. I removed my own mask, and James started guiding me slowly toward the red velvet bed with a hand on the small of my back.

James whispered, "Remember, just like we normally do. Except for this time, we have an audience."

I nodded, swallowed thickly, then walked closer to the center of the room. We stood at the footboard, and James grabbed me by the waist. He kissed me roughly, then began sucking down my neck to my chest. As he slid his tongue into my deep cleavage, I moaned but couldn't even hear myself over all the noises within the room.

James found my zipper and slowly undid my sticky leather dress. I had to help him slide it down my body because it was so tight; it kept getting caught on my breasts and butt. Carefully unzipping one boot at a time, I teetered on a heel while still attempting to look sexy.

My pulse quickened as my naked body was exposed to a room of strangers. Someone behind me was staring. I tried to turn, but my head wouldn't twist far enough to see who may be looking. James pulled my focus back to him with a kiss. I pressed into him to cover myself as much as I could.

Running my fingers up his bare chest and neck, I grasped his thick, blonde hair near the base of his skull. I helped him undress and dropped to my knees at the foot of the bed. His cock was already hard, probably from seeing Jackson fucking that other guy. The two of them finished with each other while James and I were just getting started.

Holding James' dick with one hand, I swirled my tongue around the tip, tasting his pre-cum on my tongue. He placed a hand on either side of my head, pinning it back to the bed. From this angle, he could plunge in fully and did so. I had practiced deep-throating several times but wasn't an expert. I teared up and gagged, drool running down the sides of my mouth around him.

Doing what we normally did together eased the knot in my stomach. It helped that no one seemed to be paying particular attention to us, too distracted by their own debased activities. My neck relaxed, and I could enjoy what I was doing.

James was saying things to me, but I could hardly hear him. "That's it, baby, take it." I breathed through my nose, trying to swallow him deeper.

Before he lost control, he quickly pulled out of my mouth and grasped me under my shoulders, hoisting me onto the bed. I splayed out for him on my back at the end of the mattress. Near the headboard, two men were spit-roasting a woman. One man smacked her ass from behind, pulling her hair each time he thrust forward; the other stuffed his cock down her mouth.

James kneeled on the floor to eat my pussy. I never had an orgasm from oral. It was hard enough from actual sex, but that didn't stop him from trying or me from enjoying it. My back arched like a cat as he took his first lick up my slit and settled to sucking, tongue pulsing on my clit.

I bit my knuckle to keep from crying out and turned my head to the side. When I did, I saw Xavier standing beside the fireplace, taking a sip from a double of amber-colored liquid, staring intensely at my face. As he swallowed, he pointed a finger at me with the hand that held his glass and winked. His shirt had been unbuttoned, exposing his insanely cut abs and a trail of dark hair leading below the waistline of his pants.

I tried to look away and back at James, grabbing his blonde locks and writhing my hips. He drove a finger into me, sucking on my clit. I shut my eyes until curiosity got the better of me and opened them again to see if Xavier was still looking.

He was.

This time, however, I was entranced by his gaze. As I humped James' head and moaned, I kept my eyes locked on Xavier's, showing him how much pleasure my boyfriend was giving me. Xavier stood motionless against the wall, one leg crossed over the other, his glass held low in one hand, the other holding his waistband.

Ever so subtly, Xavier opened his mouth, letting his tongue just graze over his bottom lip. At that vision and the fantasy that Xavier's tongue could be grazing over my own lips right now, I came all over James' face.

"Fuck, babe. I did it! You came!" James peeked up at me from between my legs, so proud of himself. I sat up as James stood to lean over for a kiss. I glanced to see if Xavier was watching, but he had disappeared from his spot.

James walked to a condom bowl nearby to grab one, then switched places with me, saying, "Fuck, I'm hard. Come ride my cock."

He ripped open the package, and I straddled him while he slipped the condom on. He knew I never had sex without one. Squatting up and down a few times, I slid myself onto his waiting dick. I settled in, grinding my core against his pubic bone each time I sat down.

A hard body pressed into my back, and I sat up straight. Large hands tapped open James' thighs and squirted a bottle of liquid. James smiled at whoever was behind me. I looked over my shoulder. Xavier was rolling on a condom, dribbling lube over my boyfriend's ass. He began to finger fuck James who moaned beneath me, eyes half shut with pleasure.

Xavier pulled me back into his chest with his arm tight around my waist, leaned into my ear, and said in a low deep voice, "Mind if I join you?" He smelled of the deep woods, rugged and with a hint of whiskey. My stomach did a little flip.

Xavier continued his finger assault on James before James almost choked on his tongue while yelling, "Fuck, man! Oh my god, that feels amazing!" James had just been penetrated.

Xavier worked behind me, each thrust of his hips hitting my ass with a tiny smack of our skin, which sent sparks of electricity up my spine. He tightened the arm around my waist. With his other hand, he grabbed my neck, fingers spreading over my skin. Suckling on my ear lobe, he kissed down the column of my neck, pausing just over my carotid pulse. There he bit down before easing the pain with a swirl of his tongue, then taking my skin inside his mouth with more pressure. I ground my hips harder into James, gripping him with my thighs.

"Yeah, man, fuck me into her…." James said breathlessly to Xavier. Xavier pushed in harder, our skin sticking together each time. His hand holding my neck moved to grasp my round bottom, lightly patting it as if he were prepping it for a smack or just experiencing the weight of it.

Xavier pulled away from me, his grip loosening for a moment. He turned his head to the right and shouted, "Jack... Alex..." He nodded toward the bed.

At their president's command, Jackson Riley and the man he had been fucking earlier came over to us and scooted into positions on either side of James' face. Each knelt next to his head and stroked their hard cocks. Then, Jackson began to feed his dick to my boyfriend. After a few licks and sucks, James turned his head as the other man stuck himself in James' mouth. James continued that way, suckling one, then the other, each man fondling himself when not occupying James' mouth.

Xavier fucked James with vigor. He gripped my hips with his large hands as he did, pulling me close to his body. When I leaned into him, Xavier's sweat coated my back. In a low voice, he spoke directly over my ear. "You see your boyfriend there taking all this dick? He loves it. He loves sucking cock, taking it up the ass." Xavier pounded my boyfriend more to demonstrate as James moaned around Jackson's dick.

James paused his sucking to look at me. "Oh, fuck, baby, I love cock in my ass. Fuck, I love cock." Then he returned to his blowjobs. James looked to be in a heightened state of ecstasy, but whenever he would open his mouth to yell, Jackson stuck his dick inside. James sucked hard, looking Jackson in the eyes.

Xavier worked me by guiding my hips on James' dick before whispering, "Pretty sure he's not going to be bi after tonight…" I gasped. "He can't fuck you like you need to be fucked. He's not even going to make you come." Xavier spanked my ass and drove into James with a punch of his hips.

"He-he made me come tonight," I breathed, turning my head towards Xavier. My lips tingled at how close they were to his.

Xavier let out a soft chuckle, his warm breath tickling my mouth. "Oh, *he* did? You sure about that?" Xavier's icy blue eyes turned dark as he narrowed his lids and raged into James.

"Fuck, man, fuck, you hit my spot… Oh, fuck!" James lifted his hips into me, filling the condom with hot cum.

Xavier yanked himself out of my boyfriend and ripped off his condom, throwing it to the floor. He picked me up by the waist off James' spent dick, turning my body to face him. My legs naturally encircled his waist as his erection split my wet pussy lips. My arms latched around his neck for stability. Forced against the wall next to the bed, Xavier held my bent legs wide open with his rippled forearms. His intense eyes captured mine when he shoved his entire length inside of me.

I screamed. Xavier was so much bigger than any cock I had experienced. The fullness was shocking; I stretched further than I knew possible. Xavier moved like a madman, rapidly fucking me into the wall, burrowing his face into my neck. Perspiration formed on his sculpted back where my nails dug in, holding on for dear life as his body smashed into mine.

I glanced at the bed where James was recovering from his orgasm. Jackson had taken over Xavier's place. He slid on top of my boyfriend, the two face to face, staring into each other's eyes. They began kissing, and James let his hands caress Jackson's back and head. The intimacy they shared made me look away and close my eyes.

"Open your fucking eyes," Xavier growled at me. I did and met his severe expression. "You deserve so much more."

I could see exactly how powerful this man's body was. Xavier had an intricate display of tattoos, some running up his neck and down his sculpted chest, with almost full sleeves on each corded arm.

Xavier saw me looking at his body and lifted the corners of his mouth. He dipped his head in a bob towards mine, backed away for a moment, looking at my lips as if reconsidering or making sure of his own mindful presence. Then, he claimed me with his mouth.

I tasted sweet bourbon as he sent his tongue on a mission to toy with mine. He sucked my lips, bit once, then plunged with his tongue like he was trying to get deeper inside me. My pussy pinched his thick cock, and the heat rose between my thighs. He stopped kissing to look where our bodies were joined and circled my clit with his thumb.

"He can't make you come, but you will come for me." He studied my face and then placed his forehead on mine. "You will always come for me... This pussy will be mine; I'll own it. I'll own you."

I froze. Xavier wasn't wearing a condom. He was the

first man to ever enter me without one. The thought that he would spray his cum inside me, along with how his cock stretched me and the warmth of his gravelly voice, made me come so hard I almost fainted. It wasn't just the one; I had a chain of orgasms, each leading into the next for what felt like minutes.

"That's it… that's my kitten. Come for me." Xavier whispered, heated breath on my ear as I was rolling through pulsating waves of pleasure.

Xavier deepened and slowed his pumps, scooping his hips at the end of his thrusts. My entire body turned to liquid and almost oozed down the wall when he picked up his pace with deep plunges. I understood what was about to happen too late.

"No, no, wait—" I managed to whisper to him.

Xavier bit my neck, then sucked there just above my collarbone. He yelled into my skin as he spurted hot cum inside me. "Mmm, kitten. There'll be no waiting with you. Fuck, you're mine now."

He pinned me harder to the wall and leaned in to kiss me. His lips were gentler, breaking with soft breaths in my open mouth. I tried not to kiss him back but gave in for a moment before dipping my chin to move away.

I wiggled in his hold. He dropped my legs, and I stood on shaky knees. Shoving him away from me, Xavier's amused expression worsened my irritation. "You're mad I gave you the best orgasms of your life?"

I huffed and whispered harshly, "You should have worn a condom!" His cum drizzled out of me and ran down both thighs. I hoped James didn't see.

"That will not be happening. I only fuck you raw."

He said it as if our rendezvous was to be a regular occurrence in his schedule. The only thing that quieted the fear within me was that he had to have a clean bill of health for the party, right?

"I have a boyfriend. You know, James? My boyfriend? You can't be just… taking me like that when he's right there." I threw a thumb in the direction of the bed.

Xavier didn't even move his head and stared right at me. "He's right where now?"

I glanced over, but the bed was empty. My chest was tight. Where was my boyfriend? I looked around the room. I also didn't see Jackson. I couldn't breathe. *Oh my god*! Xavier's bedroom was clearing out. What time was it?

Heaving Xavier's almost immobile chest, I managed to sneak by. Unable to stand my body's exposure, I scanned the room with desperation. I needed to find James, my clothes, and get the hell out of Xavier's bedroom.

"Where are you going?" He turned and began picking up his clothes from the floor. The last few people quickly left through the door until he and I were alone.

Frantically, I searched for my dress and boots but couldn't find them; my purse was also missing. Everything had been at the foot of the bed, but no longer. James' clothes were also gone. "I'm looking for my clothes."

Xavier had dressed in his gray trousers, leaving his tattooed chest exposed, still covered with a sheen of sweat. He walked through a door near the bathroom that I could only assume to be a closet. When he returned, he had my dress and boots lain across his arms. "These what you were looking for?"

I ran to him and reached out to snag my items, but he turned slightly, so I couldn't. "Give them to me," I said, putting my hands on my hips. My face was hot.

Xavier leered at my body. "I'm not sure I want you to get dressed yet." He bit his lip and hummed in approval. "You look like you're dying to clean up, though, so take these and use my bathroom... through there."

He handed over my clothes and boots, then pointed to the bathroom door. I snatched them, scurrying off, and he chortled behind me.

After cleaning up, I returned to the room. Xavier was lying on his side on the rumpled bed. He patted the mattress beside him. I rolled my eyes and said, "I have to find James. Did you see where he went?" I twisted my fingers together and searched the room for my purse.

"Sure did. He left with Jackson earlier. Think they headed downstairs with the others."

"Well, then I'll just..." I slinked by the bed, then stopped. "Have you seen my purse?" I asked him while scanning the room to avoid his intense eyes.

Xavier reached behind him and showed the little bag, holding it out to me. I approached with caution, hoping it wasn't a trick. But, before I could grab it, he moved the clutch out of my reach and pulled on my arm to draw me closer as he sat up. Our faces were almost touching.

"I need you to understand something. I wasn't

fucking around, Marissa. You're mine now. If you want to interrupt your little friend so he can take you home, that's fine. For tonight. Understand, though, you have a week to end things... or I will." Xavier placed my beaded evening bag in my open palm and let go of my arm. I stumbled back with my mouth wide open.

"End things? You mean, with my boyfriend, with James?" Was this man insane? He thought he could fuck me in front of my boyfriend without a condom and demand I break up with him? I squinted at him. "Who do you think you are?"

"The man who owns you now, kitten. So be a good girl and break things off before next Saturday." Xavier stood and gathered me tightly to his bare chest. He lifted my chin and kissed me deeply. When he gave me a little space, I broke his hold. As I turned to run, he spanked my ass hard and chuckled.

"Night, kitten."

Chapter Three

THE DISCOVERY

Fleeing Xavier's room, I tried to remember the path we had taken when we arrived. After a few wrong turns and an almost panic attack, I found my way to the entrance hall and looked around. The house was still packed with people. I looked in each of the rooms downstairs, but couldn't find James. I was helpless without my phone.

Several times in my flustered dash around the house, a man would stop me, asking if I was down to fuck. I quickly made excuses and passed them. Once, a frat brother wouldn't take no for an answer and threw me over his shoulder. Fortunately, after beating him with my bag, he dropped me and laughed while walking away, shaking his head.

On a rushed scan through a less crowded hallway, I saw the redhead in leopard print lingerie exit a bathroom. She eyed me up and down with an eyebrow arched, then flipped her hair over one shoulder.

"Scared, little girl?" She sneered.

"Uh, have you seen James, my boyfriend?" I had done something to piss this woman off, but hopefully, she'd still give me information.

"James is *your* boyfriend? Well, I think he's with Jackson." She brushed past me and wiggled her hips down the hall. So James *was* with Jackson. I swallowed to help with nausea rising from my stomach.

Rushing to the rooms on the other side of the first story, I tried to recognize anyone to help me. Alex, one of the men James sucked off, was leaning against a wall in a hall between the dining room and what may have been the kitchen. A line of women was on the opposite side, waiting for the bathroom. I ran to Alex praying he knew where James had gone.

"Oh, hey! James' girlfriend, right?" Alex snickered over the term in such a way that made me think he thought it was a big joke.

"Uh, yeah. Have you seen him?" I continued to scan the hall while asking.

Alex grinned and looked around with me, sipping his drink, "Yep. James is out back. Pretty sure he's in the pool house by now." He seemed to find my panic amusing.

"Thanks," I said as I quickly turned away.

Alex grabbed my shoulder and said, "I think I'd give him a few more minutes."

I shrugged him off and huffed. Weaving through guests, I made it to the entry. The glass doors were still open to the patio. As I walked past the pool, now filled with more partiers than fuckers, I saw a small wood-clad cottage to my left. It had to be the pool house. There were lights on inside.

I hustled to the door as much as my heeled boots would allow. As I went to open it, James said breathlessly, "Fuck, baby, you're exactly what I wanted."

"Me, too, handsome," another man said.

When I stepped inside, Jackson was leaning James' naked body against one of the beadboard walls. They were kissing and stroking each other's hardening dicks. James held Jackson close by his butt with one hand while tugging him with his other. Then, Jackson pressed their dicks in his massive hand, fondling them together.

"*Fuuuck*, baby." James leaned back and closed his eyes. I must have made a noise because both stopped moving and snapped their heads at me.

"Oh, fuck. Jackson, stop. Marissa? I thought you were upstairs. Uh... baby, hold on, wait, stop." Jackson paused his strokes for a second, noticed me over his shoulder, then started grinding on James. He grasped James' face with his hand, shoving his tongue inside his mouth.

Jackson stopped their kissing only long enough to say loudly, "James is busy, sweetheart." He returned to sucking my boyfriend's face. James began pumping his cock in Jackson's hand, threw his arms around his neck, and kissed him back, groaning. I stood there another minute with my mouth open, watching as they enjoyed each other.

Almost tripping over myself, I ran out of the cottage to the pool area. My heart and sanity started to break. This wasn't part of our plan; our rules had been destroyed. We weren't supposed to have sex with other people alone, and now we both had. My skin felt dirty, used.

Desperate to get out, I ran my fingers through my hair and pulled. I didn't want to cry in front of all these strangers. How was I supposed to get home? I had no phone, and the only other person I sort of knew was the psychotic president of this madhouse. As I started calculating how long it would take to walk back to civilization, I was grabbed in a tight embrace, and a high-pitched squeal met my ears.

"Oh, my god. You were invited, too? And you showed up?" Elle's beautiful figure stood in front of me in a tiny white string bikini. "I have so much to tell you."

I had never been more grateful to see one of my friends. "Elle?"

When I looked at her, Elle dropped her smile. "Fuck. What happened? Are you okay? You need help?"

The tears flowed. "He called him 'baby.'"

"Shit…" Elle glanced around, then held me closer to her. "We need to get out of here, don't we?"

I nodded as I put my head into her blonde hair. She led me around the pool area while she seemed to make some goodbye excuses to whomever she had been hooking up with, grabbing her purse and clothes. I was so out of it, I don't remember any faces as she tugged me towards the entry and out front towards the fountain.

"Neon green Porsche. You can't miss it," she said to the valet. My eyes wouldn't focus. A sob escaped my mouth. "Shh, shh, just a sec, and we'll be home." Elle rubbed my back, her arm around me, pressing my face into her neck. She checked to ensure I still had my purse before we got into her obnoxiously painted sports car.

As soon as we got in, she asked, "What happened?"

I sniffed. "James doesn't want me anymore. I think... I'm pretty sure tonight was what I knew it would be. He used this as his way of 'exploring' away from me."

"You mean he and Jackson?" She tilted her head and squinted her eyes.

"Did you know?"

"Um, promise you won't hate me. I introduced Jackson and James a few months ago. Jackson made it clear he wanted James for himself. I saw them come downstairs naked together tonight, but I thought... Well, I thought maybe you were okay with it, you know, the whole 'exploration' thing." She paused. "I mean, I was going to mention it to you tomorrow, but we aren't supposed to talk about what happens at Red Night without getting offed or something."

I let the image of Jackson and James together flash over my mind again. Pain wrapped around my chest. "No, no, I don't blame you at all. You rescued me. I think–I think this has been coming for a while."

"Talk with James, Marissa. Maybe he's just high or something. I'm sure you guys will work it out." She seemed to think about what she was saying, then added, "But if he did fuck around on you, I will cut off his balls myself."

When we arrived back at the apartment, Sharice was still awake, meal-prepping at the kitchen island. She saw my face, put her knife down, and grabbed a bottle of wine from the refrigerator. "Shit. What happened?" She grabbed three glasses from the cabinet. Elle and I sat on the living room sofa, and Sharice came over to squat in front of us, medicine in hand.

I sniffed. "James had sex with Jackson Riley. I tried to interrupt them, but he ignored me and kept going."

"Damn it. Do we even need the glasses?" Sharice turned on the Bluetooth speaker to a heavy metal playlist. Being a music major, she always knew which music fit each mood. Filling the glasses, she handed one to each of us and set the bottle on the glass coffee table.

The three of us ordered trash food, drank wine, and complained about men until Kinsley came home from a terrible date to join us. Of course, being my closest friends, they all told me to dump James, that he was no good, that I could do better... They all loved him, despite what they said. Most everyone did.

"You said James and Jackson were making out in a bedroom. Did you mean Xavier Cardell's room?" Elle asked, her eyes narrowed.

"Uh, yeah." I wanted to avoid the topic of Xavier.

"Oh, wow. I heard he only lets certain people in. What happened in there? A watercolor picture of events is fine. Like if you knew anyone else."

I explained the scene to Elle since she had an invite, telling Kins and Sharice to "keep your ears shut" since I was technically not allowed to say.

"Did—did *you* end up with anyone there?" Kinsley asked with her eyebrows up and a smile on her face.

"Um. Well, I don't think I should say any details. We

could get in trouble. You know, like Elle said." My room-mates nodded, but Elle shot me a glance.

I showered and got ready for bed. There was a knock on the bathroom door I shared with Elle. Her bedroom was next to mine. Across the apartment, past the open common area, were identical rooms for Sharice and Kinsley. I opened the door and stepped back.

"Who was it?" Elle grinned as if she knew my secret.

"Who was what?" I asked innocently.

"Stop playing. Who did you hook up with?"

"James, who also hooked up with Jackson. I told you."

"Did you hook up with Xavier Cardell?" She asked me, furrowing her brow.

"Wh-why do you say that?" My face got hot.

"Ah-ha! I *knew* it. You're going to get married and have his babies. I can tell."

"What?! You're crazy."

"He asked about you freshman year. I think he was trying to hook up with you then, but you were already into James."

"Really? When?" Ugh. Why did I sound eager?

"It was early on after you and James started hooking up, I think."

"What did he say?" *And please include tone and intonation.*

"I don't remember. That was two years ago, and I was probably drunk." Elle started to put toothpaste on her toothbrush. I sighed and walked to my room.

"Wait!" She stopped me. "He asked something

weird, like if you were from around here and if I knew your dad's name, but I didn't."

"My dad's name? Like his first name?"

She shrugged and put the toothbrush in her mouth. "I guess."

"Huh… well, goodnight." That was strange.

Sliding between my gray sheets, I was prepared to surrender to my wine buzz. Instead, I tossed and turned, thinking about the events of the evening. My mind brought up the image of James and Jackson on the bed, in the pool house, but worst of all was the image of the intensity of Xavier's eyes while he was inside of me. The taste of his tongue and the smell of his body. Remembering the feel of his mouth over my ear while he spoke those words to me.

The ones that stuck out the most were about deserving something more and that I was now his. Xavier didn't even know me; how did he know what I deserved? Why was he asking Elle about me *two years ago* when he hadn't so much as glanced in my direction?

Despite my shower, I still felt his big hands on my body and his cum between my thighs. Like muscle memory, my pussy pulsed, thinking of how much he stretched me. I was grateful to be on the pill, but that didn't negate the fact that he could have given me something. He was a player. What if he used those lines on other girls; refused to wear a condom? I planned to go to student health and get tested again.

Whimpering, I finally fell asleep and did not awaken until late into Sunday. I tried to lay in bed as long as possible, not wanting to wake up and feel the pain and anger anymore. I had expected James to come through my balcony in the middle of the night or at least try to call, but he never did. Maybe he didn't have his phone because he was still at the TRZ house... with Jackson.

Worried, I scrolled through social media on my laptop while lying in bed to see if anyone knew where he was. Fortunately, there weren't any pictures from Red Night, but I found Jackson Riley's account. My body froze when I saw his latest picture posted an hour before.

Jackson was lying on a couch in a room I didn't recognize, but a bed was in the background. He was shirtless, his legs propped up on a coffee table with two plates of pancakes. The top of a blonde head was resting in Jackson's lap. The caption was: *Brunch Sunday morning with the boy *heart emoji**. It was James.

Comments on his picture included people saying, "Finally!" and "I knew it!" and "You guys are so great together!" I rolled over on my side and cried.

Chapter Four

BEGINNINGS AND ENDINGS

I must have fallen asleep but a pleasurable sensation arose between my legs. Someone's head was resting on my pussy. A sleepy moan escaped my lips at the tongue lapping my clit, while thick fingers dipped inside me.

Did James think he could lick me awake and things would be fine between us? I tried to buck the head off me, but sturdy hands clasped my legs to pry them open and shove me down. I whimpered as the tongue flicked my clit harder, slurping sounds echoing between my thighs.

I opened my eyes just as I was about to come. The head of someone with sleek black hair was eating me like a ravaging beast. Icy blue eyes met mine as his fingers plunged deeper inside, and my rapture escalated.

"Come for me, kitten," Xavier said against my clit. I gripped his silky strands with my hands and his face with my thighs as I reached ecstasy. He hummed against my pussy, then sat up at the end of my bed and pulled his thick hard cock out from his black sweat-pants, giving it a couple of jerks with his hand. I was stark naked.

"You taste amazing." Xavier licked around his full bottom lip, gathering up my juices as he moved closer to put his long cock inside me. Now that I could see it, I gasped at its thickness.

"Wha-what are you doing here?" I tried to back up on my elbows to my headboard.

Xavier tilted his head in confusion. "Fucking my girl. Slide down here."

"N-no, you're not. I'm not your girl!"

"You came like my good girl."

"I thought you were James."

Xavier's brow wrinkled then he snorted. "James could never eat your pussy like that, kitten. Open up for me. Show me who this pussy belongs to." He leaned over my body and started to stick his dick inside me. I clenched.

"Wait, Xavier. Wait."

"Told you there's no waiting with you." He plunged in, and I bucked against him. This crazy man broke into my room, ate my pussy, and was fucking me raw, saying I was his girl.

As he grunted and thrust deep strokes inside me, I was desperate to make him stop. I wasn't a cheater, not like James. Having sex with Xavier in front of James last night was one thing, but the following day? Not during a Red Night? That was wrong.

Despite knowing that logically, his body was doing incredible things to me physically. I moaned and arched into him, grinding my hips to meet his. I shouldn't want this.

"I can't. Oh, fuck… I can't cheat on James. This… mmm… this is wrong." I tried to maintain some clarity, but Xavier made rational thought difficult. He leaned down to my breasts and latched onto one nipple with his mouth and then the other. Watching my face, he bit down on one before tracing it with the tip of his tongue. I yelled and clamped down on his thick cock.

"Hmm, we'll have to get these pierced," he said. "Maybe your clit, too? Would my kitten like jewelry?"

He pushed his hips to hold me down when I tried to buck against him again. "Xavier, I can't do this. I'm not a cheater." I was panting, writhing, moaning, sweating.

"You aren't a cheater now 'cause you're mine. Your body's begging for this big cock. Look at you, beautiful. You're a mess for it."

"I'm not begging—Oh, fuck." I was falling over the edge, fire burning me inside. I cried tears of joy. "Please, please, please. Right there. Don't stop. Don't stop. Don't —" I came so hard my legs started to convulse. I may have squirted if he hadn't been buried inside me.

While my pussy was still pulsing, I wrapped my legs around him and dug my feet into his ass to get him as deep inside me as I could. His cock throbbed, his face tensed as he held mine, and he came with a loud groan that turned into my name.

Xavier went into a frenzy on me: kissing my lips, grabbing my hair, sucking my neck, still trying to empty his cock, squeezing out any drops of cum he could. Our faces pressed close as he poked another mini-pump inside, half lying on top of me. Inhaling deeply, he lightly touched a palm to my cheek and stared at me.

"*Fuck*, Marissa. I can't leave this pussy. I may have to stay here all day and continue to pump you full the rest of the night." He thrust his hips. "You got any snacks in here?" He glanced around the room, holding one forearm behind my neck.

"Xavier, what the fuck? Get off me." I shoved him. His spent cock slipped out as his cum and mine started to pour out of me. "I don't know what kind of game you're playing, but it's wrong. I have a boyfriend."

"Not playing a game. And you do have a boyfriend —me." He was lying on his side with his sweatpants down, showcasing his large, flaccid dick. He smiled sweetly, reaching to tug on a piece of my hair, stroking it gently while I sat on the bed in front of him.

"James is my boyfriend. You just made me a cheater. I can't believe you did that."

Xavier chuckled. "Yeah, that was all on me… 'Please, please. Don't stop. Don't stop.'" He mocked my voice. "Wrapping your legs around me so you could get more of my cum… Kitten, if you want a litter, I'll be happy to get started now."

"You're twisted. What is wrong with you? A month ago, I didn't even think you knew my name… Now, what, you think you're my boyfriend?"

"I am your boyfriend. Told you. I own you."

My mouth fell open and a million retorts flooded my mind. *Own* me? How dare he?

Before I could choose a coherent reply Xavier sat up and took my trembling hand. "I've known about you a long time, Marissa Matlock. Born the only child of Rodney and Susan Matlock, who both attended Northview University, where they met and married right after graduation. You came along soon after, born on March fifteenth. Beware the Ides."

I scrambled off the bed, horrified that this man seemed to have memorized a people finder page of facts about me. Quickly, I pulled on an old T-shirt from the floor and some sleep shorts. Couldn't find my panties.

"How—what are you doing?!" I stood back from the bed. I would have to cross him to escape the room.

Xavier casually pulled up his sweatpants and laid down, arms folded behind his head on the pillow. He seemed to settle into my bed as if it were his own.

"In elementary school, your best friend, Essa, had to move away when her mother got cancer. You vowed never to have another friend. You spent your days after school painting, taking pictures with your dad's old Nikon camera."

"Stop, please. Is this a sick joke?" My face felt hot.

"Your uncle tried to ruin you when you were in middle school, but you screamed and ran away. You told your dad, who beat him to a pulp, sending him to the hospital. He still has a limp but is in prison for hurting other little girls."

"Stop. I'm begging you. How do you know this stuff about me, Xavier?" I panted shaky breaths, wringing my hands. I was horrified. Even James didn't know this stuff about me. Other than my family, I don't think anyone knew some of these things.

"In high school, Evan stole your virginity from me.

He lasted less than a minute, and you wondered, '*Is this what all the hype has been about?*'"

My diaries. This fucker has read my diaries... My old diaries, though. Like the ones still at my parents' house, not here in this apartment. My stomach flipped.

I whispered mainly to myself, "You read my diaries. How did you get to them?"

"Freshman year, you were at the Delta party when some guy tried to put something in your cup, but *Trevor*," he said the name with disgust, "held his hand over your drink and said he would watch out for you. Little did you know it was just a stupid pick-up game pledges played to hit on girls. Waste of a scrotum couldn't even get you to orgasm."

"Xavier! How did you get them?"

With the panic in my voice, he brought his legs up, resting his arms against his knees. "Kitten, you're mine. I know everything about you. Besides, Mom filled in any details the diaries left out."

"M-mom?"

"Yeah, Susan? Mom? Well, she asked me if I would call her that since I'd be her son-in-law and all. She wants us to come to dinner Wednesday, by the way. She's mad you didn't tell her about me."

"What? What are you talking about? When did you meet my mother?" Bile was rising in my throat.

"This morning, I stopped by to introduce myself and chat since we're official now. She made me tea, showed me your room... I'm a fast reader." He leaned back again and grinned, opening a palm towards my recent diaries near my desk.

This man was insane. How was I supposed to get a large unstable man out of my bedroom? He had spoken with my mother. Even if he hadn't explicitly said it, he made a veiled threat at James. If he knew my diaries, he knew all my deepest secrets. Gripping my T-shirt, I pulled it down to cover my body as if he could see through the shield of my clothing.

"I want you to leave." I made my voice firm but wanted to vomit and run.

"Yeah, I thought we'd go get some food. I'm hungry. I'm sure you're starving. Did you even eat today, kitten?" Xavier got off the bed and grabbed a hoodie from the floor, pulling it over his head. He tugged on socks and a pair of running shoes.

I didn't know how to get out of this. "Why do you keep calling me kitten?"

"Your kitten mask… from Red Night." He tsked at me as if that was a thousand nights before last.

"Please leave."

"We are leaving; we're going to get food. Come on." He held his hand out to me impatiently. "Get your purse." Then he beckoned me towards the door with his head.

"Xavier, I'm not going anywhere with you."

There was a knock on the door. Kinsley spoke from the other side, "Marissa, will you two quit fucking long enough to come out with us?"

Shit, she thought James was here… "Just a minute!" I yelled. "You need to go." I directed Xavier toward my open balcony with a pointed finger and a sharp glare.

"Guys… come on! It's been hours. Aren't you sore?" Kinsley whined.

"Please, please, Xavier. Please go." I begged, water coming to my eyes.

Xavier's face softened from his standard smirky grin as he saw my tears. He padded to me, taking my face in his hands and lifting it so I had to stare into those ice eyes. "You have six days. We have a function to attend on Saturday night." He placed his lips to mine, then left my room through the balcony.

I wanted to crumple to the floor. Instead, I marched over to the door and opened it. Kinsley was still on the other side, irritated with "us" taking so long. Elle was on the sofa applying some toenail polish. Sharice was studying at the dining room table.

"Holy shit, he must have fucked you good. Where is he?" Kinsley gasped when she saw me.

"Oh, um, he sneaked out the balcony."

"Why? Oh, well. He was invited to get food with us… I guess we can do it another time. You want to get ready and go? College pizza night at Tony's!"

Hunger filled my belly now that I had escaped from my stalker. I tidied up in the bathroom, then headed to my room to change. My phone vibrated with an incoming text and dinged from a missed voicemail message.

I quickly grabbed it from my dresser. While asleep, I missed a text from my mother asking why I had not introduced her to "your new boyfriend." She also left a voicemail, shocked that I hadn't told them, and asked, "What happened with James?"

I saw a few missed texts and a voicemail from James, which were left while Xavier was inside me.

JAMES

Baby im so sry just got my phone

RU home? I'm coming over.

Please call me.

This had been sent just after the voicemail message while I was in the bathroom. I listened:

"Marissa, I am in my car, outside your apartment. I just came over to crawl in bed with you, figured you were asleep... [deep breath here]. What in the actual fuck was Xavier Cardell doing in your room? Don't deny it. I saw him through the balcony. Is that why you're not answering me? Jackson said he saw you two last night. Told me you've had something going on... Is that true? Marissa, please. What is going on? Please call me, text me, something! I'm desperate."

Jackson... What gives James the right to be mad about Xavier? I may have been thrown into sex with Xavier while James was in the room, but he went off with Jackson alone.

After Xavier had quieted any lingering negative emotions by giving me an amazing orgasm, my anger was starting to return. I couldn't talk to James while I was this infuriated. I texted him to tell him I was safe and would be heading to Tony's and told him we could talk later. He agreed to meet me as soon as I got home.

After great pizza and several beers, my rage and pain were lessened to irritation and a steady ache. I texted James to come over. He said he'd be there right away. I told the girls I'd be okay and wasn't exactly sure what would happen. Things weren't looking too good for James and James' girlfriend.

James arrived a few minutes later, looking incredibly hung over. Dark circles sagged underneath his eyes, and his normally styled hair was disheveled. He shuffled inside the apartment, sheepishly grinning at my room-mates, probably knowing we'd all been talking about him. When he got to my room, he went to the balcony and began to pace. He wasn't touching me. Either he was mad or...

"Marissa, I fucked up. Last night, today... Maybe for the last few months. I'm fucked up." James sighed deeply, staring at the ceiling, and I waited for him to continue. "You know I've been obsessed with Jackson... I... *fuck*. I slept with him last night during Red Night, well, you saw us. The pool house was fucked up. I was fucked up on Molly. I went to his room with him last night—we didn't do anything there, I swear. It's why—it's why I didn't have my phone. I fucked up, baby." He choked out the last words, barely looking at me as he spoke.

White-hot anger bubbled up and out through my voice. "Don't call me baby. You called him that. I heard you in the pool house."

"You fucked Xavier Cardell! You have *no* room to talk! I fucking *saw* you, Marissa! At least you knew Jackson and I were together, and it was just Red Night. We had rules!"

"Xavier fucked you, too! He basically threw himself on me at the party."

"But he was here today. I saw him! I saw him through the window and was so fucking pissed off I left." He stopped yelling and got quieter. "Maybe I was pissed off at what I did to lead you to him last night… the pool house. I'm so fucking sorry, but how could you be with him today? Did you want revenge? You wanted to hurt me?"

"I thought he was you! I didn't know he was going to show up here. I was half asleep!"

"So he raped you."

I paused. "Um, well, not exactly."

"Marissa, did he force himself on you? *Did you tell him no?*"

I looked at my hands. I knew I hadn't. Fuck Xavier. He was right; I had wanted it. James blew out a huge breath and sat on my bed, head in his hands.

"It's me. I've been on this quest of discovery and left you behind; I know it. I'm so sorry, Marissa. I'm getting pissed off about Xavier when I—"

I stood in front of him at the end of the bed. Taking one of his hands in mine, I said quietly, "I think the party was a mistake."

"Yeah… maybe it was." James sighed, then squeezed my hand. He pulled me into him, wrapped his arm around my waist, and pressed his head into my stomach.

"Marissa, I love you, but I'm having a hard time right now. I feel confused."

My breath caught. "Confused about what?"

"About, I don't know… Can we forget last night happened and go back to Friday?" He looked at my face, raising his eyebrows.

I considered this. If I forgot about the party, we could go back to the way things were. I would be James' girlfriend, and he would... continue to pursue Jackson or some other man. Part of me was desperate to forget that Saturday ever happened, but I knew I couldn't.

"I'm not sure I can do that. The way Jackson spoke to me, and you just let him. You kept fucking him, James! You went to his room last night!"

James stood, wrapped both arms around me, and burrowed his face into my hair. "I am so fucking sorry, Marissa." He was crying. "I'm confused. Maybe I am gay. I'm not sure. I think last night was a mistake. I shouldn't have used that to figure out my head. I should never have used you to figure things out for myself."

"I'm sorry, too, James. I shouldn't have had sex with him." I hugged him tighter.

"I think I need some time away. From the romance," James said. He stared at me desperately. "Marissa, I can't lose you. I can't not have you in my life." His eyes were filled with tears, and my cheeks were wet with mine.

I nodded but could barely speak. Finally, I squeaked out, "I can't lose you, either."

"Damn it; I may have just fucked up the best thing that ever happened to me."

"Or you could be figuring out the best thing for you," I said. The words were for me as much as for him.

James held me for a while longer. He said he needed a break from our relationship to figure things out but wanted to hang out as friends. I said I would when I could without feeling so hurt. He understood, saying he felt the same.

"Um... do you want me to stay and hold you tonight?" James looked hopeful.

I sighed. Part of me did, for comfort, but the wise part of me knew it would hurt when he left in the morning without us having sex like normal. Or worse, actually having sex and regretting it.

"No, I think it's best for me to sleep alone."

He nodded slowly, released me from his grip, then walked out my door, wiping his eyes. Despite the pain of watching him go, that logical part of my brain knew it was right for me. And for James as well. I lay on the bed and cried about losing everything I had known for the last two years, possibly even losing a friend.

Chapter Five

A LESSON

That night, I locked my balcony and pulled the blackout curtains. On top of schoolwork and dealing with a breakup, I had no brain energy left to consider how to handle my stalker. I would have to spend time thinking up a plan, eventually.

After only a few hours of rest, I was awake again. Visions of James and Jackson together caused me to wrestle with the sheets. But then, memories of Xavier's thick cock inside me would interrupt those thoughts, and I would get aroused. My cheeks flamed, picturing Xavier reading all my diaries, knowing my family's dark secret: my uncle, the child rapist.

I kicked around in bed with this cycle of images and thoughts repeatedly playing until I decided to give up on trying to sleep. It was only 4 a.m. when I checked the time on my phone, the sun not yet peaking. Dressed in my NU sweatshirt and matching sweatpants, I walked to my little art studio assigned to me by the university.

Outside most of the rooms, student artists exhibited

their proud work in glass displays located in the halls of the art building. Our professors often signed positive reviews underneath the piece, showcasing the artist's strengths. The wall outside my room was empty.

We were assigned something in oils this week. I also needed to brainstorm ideas for my photography project due at the end of the semester. Fortunately, I had already written my paper for my Art History class before the party, so some of my work for the week was already completed.

I placed an earbud into each ear and selected a classical music playlist on my phone (Beethoven's Sonata Number 17); it always helped me work. I gathered my supplies, donned my apron, and pulled out a canvas.

After finishing the rest of the canvas prep, I lined out my colors with dark grays and blues, leading to peaks of reds and browns and ending with deep greens and creams near the bottom. As I brushed, I remembered the anxiety from Saturday night. Some lust and passion were twisted in the colors there, too. Finally, I let the hurt and pain take me so I could feel it all.

Stopping to blow my nose a few times, I paused my process to cry, but I pressed on. Over the next couple of hours, I set the scene for my painting. The colors showed a shadow of a little girl standing before a large, intimidating castle lit only by moonlight. Near the door was a beckoning lighted figure outlined in red. In a window above was a shadow outlined in white.

It was almost time to get ready for my first class; my stomach growled. I had been working for hours. Jogging back to the apartment, I showered, dressed, and grabbed some coffee. Darling Sharice always stocked our fridge with healthy foods. Today there was a pan of protein bars inside with a sticky note that said, "Eat Me." So I did.

With the painting well underway, food in my belly, and clean clothes, I was emotionally stronger. Pouring some pain into the paint also helped. I hoped I wouldn't run into many people asking about James today. I especially didn't want to see Jackson… or Xavier. Usually, I did not cross paths with them on campus.

After morning classes, I avoided the quad (and James) for lunch, opting for the grab-and-go boxes in the cafeteria. I ate it outside the door to my last class, photography with Mr. Hall. As he approached, Mr. Hall's eyebrows raised. His body loomed over me while I slumped on the floor, leaning against the wall.

"Ms. Matlock, good to see you. We should discuss your semester project this afternoon. Are you free right after class?" he asked as if he didn't already know; it was the time we usually met so he could berate my work.

"Um, yeah… I'm free then. I have some ideas of what I'd like to do." I didn't, but I hoped to think of something during class.

In the auditorium, I sat next to Madison, another photography major. I glanced over her notebook as she took scribbled notes. Was it possible to cheat on your project ideas like it was an exam? Madison always had positive comments written under her works, even from Mr. Hall. I was betting she already had her project completed for the year.

I whispered in her light brown hair, "Hey, sorry. Do

you already know what you're going to do for your
semester project?"

"Yeah. I started on it last week. Why?"

Figured. "Oh, no reason. Just trying to come up with
ideas."

"You should talk with Mr. Hall. He's *very* helpful
with that kind of stuff. Getting you started and helping
you achieve your goals."

Mr. Hall paused his lecture and eyed us. We straightened in our seats. Madison tapped on her notebook and
wrote me a note instead. I looked at the paper where she
had written:

Have you been to his studio yet?

I shook my head at her. She wrote again:

You should go. It's very inspiring.

After the lesson, I waited outside the door for Mr.
Hall. The way he carried his tall body covered in stylish
clothes made me feel like a child as we walked to his
office on the first floor. I tried to make small talk, but he
only mumbled short replies.

Taking up my usual seat in the chair across from his
desk, Mr. Hall sat and peaked his fingers into a point in
front of his mustache, staring at me intensely. I fidgeted
in my chair, feeling uncomfortable under his scrutiny.
His gaze made me feel overexposed.

"I'm going to level with you, Ms. Matlock. I think
you have genuine, natural photographic talent. It's one

reason I want to push you so hard. However, you never put in the extra effort it takes to rise to your potential. It feels like you are waiting for something to happen instead of taking the first step yourself."

I opened my mouth in protest, but he interrupted, "—let me finish. I could help, but you must be willing to work hard and sweat a little bit. You haven't taken me up on any offers to participate at my studio, and I'm afraid if your semester project doesn't blow me away, you may fail my course." Mr. Hall lowered his head and narrowed his eyes.

He walked around his desk and leaned on it right in front of where I was sitting. His crotch was at eye level, and I could see a bulge in his corduroy pants. I was picking up on innuendos, but I wasn't sure. Was Mr. Hall... was he erect for me?

My body cringed. Looking at the bookcase behind him, I tried to ignore his stare and his crotch. "Um, I am willing to put in the work. I decided to take you up on that offer to watch you in the studio. I am available whenever you are." It was inevitable for me to visit him there; I had to pass the class.

"I'm glad to hear that. But how much energy are you willing to put in *today* to get your grade up?" With this, Mr. Hall reached out to stroke a finger along my cheek, then raised my jaw so I had to look him in the eyes.

He was being creepy. Was he going to say the actual words? Was he going to force me? If someone recorded the audio, he could easily play it off, saying he was only encouraging his student. I didn't know if he had done anything yet that I could report. I also wasn't sure if I was reading into things too much. Maybe he was trying to be kind and helpful.

Timidly, I glanced at him through my lashes. He was still towering over me, rubbing his finger underneath my jaw. I quietly breathed out, "I mean, what do I need to do to get my grade up?"

Mr. Hall reached down to his crotch and undid his pants. He pulled out his skinny, but long, hard penis. He grunted, then gripped my face, pulling me towards it. "Mmm, you want to get an A in this course? You have to get in deep. Be willing to go all in for this job." He was inching his dick closer to my face.

Those upperclassmen got stars in their eyes when talking about "visiting" Mr. Hall in his studio because they *wanted* to fuck him. He had fucked them. They got good grades. He got co-ed pussy–it was a win-win. I could do that, right? I could be one of those girls, too. I wanted an easy grade.

I licked the tip of his dick with my tongue as he dropped his head back and groaned, "That's it, Marissa. Just need you to put in a bit of extra effort." He moved his hand from my jaw to the back of my head and persuaded it to move so I'd have to take more of him.

I closed my eyes and concentrated on a mantra: I could be one of those girls... *Easy grade... Just a blowjob... Graduation...* If I did this, Mr. Hall would stop torturing me. I could hang some photos in the hall like other students. He would comment beneath, saying how amazing my collections were. People would see me as a

real photographer. Like Madison. Like the other girls…
Easy grade.

As he pushed on my head, my mouth opened, taking his cock inside. Flattening my tongue, I stroked up on the underside of the tip. I looked into his eyes, filled with a hunger for me. Just suck this dick, and I would be okay the rest of my time in university. It's not that big of a deal—just a blowjob.

Mr. Hall stepped closer and forced more of himself into my mouth, shoving more of my head onto his length. "That's it. Work hard. Mmm, Marissa, I think your grade is already improving. You definitely want that A, I can tell." Twisting my tongue around his dick, I sucked harder, taking more in because he was shoving it into me.

Mr. Hall was an attractive older man: salt and pepper hair and a good body for a forty-five to fifty-something. I could see his chest hair peeking out of his dress shirt. I could do this. I could suck him during office hours, maybe let him fuck me once. I mean, I was already doing this… I was sucking his dick; his dick was in my mouth. I was sucking my professor's dick for an A.

"I can't do this." I sat back forcibly and wiped my mouth, feeling sick. Scanning the room for a trash can, I spat out, "I just can't. I don't want this. I'm not like those girls. I can't suck you for an A. No."

When I stood, Mr. Hall grabbed me by the arms and swung me around, bending me over his desk. Holding my arms tightly behind my back, he humped my ass, still covered with tight jeans. He moved my arms from two of his hands to one, then reached around me to fumble with my button and zipper. I begged him to stop, squirming in his grip, trying to scream no. I didn't want this.

"You little cunt. Teasing me for a fucking year. You'll take my dick and thank me for your grade later." He gave up on the jeans just long enough to spank me. When he did so, I shoved back enough that he lost his balance. I grabbed my bag and ran to the door, throwing it open.

I ran down the hall and into a man's solid chest. Formidable arms enveloped me. I peered into icy blue eyes and burst into tears.

"What's wrong, beautiful?" Xavier asked, but his gaze was narrowed on Mr. Hall's open door. I turned to see Mr. Hall peak out, then observed Xavier holding me protectively before he grimaced and marched back into his office, closing the door.

Xavier snarled, "Did he hurt you?" I had seen Xavier annoyed, but the look in his eyes was downright murderous.

Snuggling closer in Xavier's embrace, I was comforted by his possessiveness for once. It was odd feeling relieved by his presence, but I was glad he was there at the right time. I didn't want to talk about what happened or what I'd have to do. Police reports, university senate talks, the gossip mills, ugh… the news? It was overwhelming; I wanted to escape.

"Please, can I just go?"

Xavier nodded in understanding and put his arm around me as we hustled out of the building to the parking lot.

Of course the heir of Cardell Enterprises would have a front-row spot in the lot when all the other off-campus plebs had to park miles away. We approached a bright blue rocket ship of a car. I was sure it was expensive, just as Xavier's clothes, watch, and backpack were. He opened the door, and the thing looked like it was going to take flight. He put me in the passenger seat, buckling my seatbelt while storing my bag in the trunk. He got in himself and closed the wing door.

"What is this thing?"

Xavier started the engine by pressing a button. As it roared to life, the power made my pussy tingle on the seat. "A Maserati MC Twenty." He noticed my reaction, glancing at my tightened thighs. "You like that?"

"It looks like a rocket ship."

"It drives like one." He flew out of his parking spot in reverse and flipped around to drive off like a stunt driver. I clutched the door, and Xavier chuckled. My reaction seemed to quell his bubbling anger, and the fear of dying in a car crash was easing mine.

Xavier drove us immediately to the backroads of town, using curvy lanes to show off his car's prowess. He reached over and grabbed my hand, which had been clutching the seat in fear. He laced our fingers together and placed them on his lap.

"So, you wanna tell me what happened back there?" Xavier glanced at me to gauge my reaction.

"Um, Mr. Hall asked me to suck his dick for an A. When I stopped him, he tried to pull down my jeans." I didn't want to look at Xavier's reaction, but I was drawn to him. His jaw was clenched as the bitter pill he sucked was more sour today. He remained quiet. I sighed. "I think I should have just gotten it over with. It's not worth the trouble."

Xavier's rage was palpable. "Excuse me? You think it would have been okay? For what, a grade? Fuck that, Marissa." He seethed and said under his breath, "He will pay."

There was heavy silence in the car, my head unable to contain the myriad of thoughts and feelings I was having. Xavier gunned the rocket after curving around a sharp corner.

"I don't even want to report it. It'll all be so draining… all the reports, the news. Maybe I can try to switch advisors again."

I tried to switch last year, but Mr. Hall intervened, saying I needed him since I was interested in portrait photography. Maybe now he would be so disgusted with me that he'd let me go. I could even blackmail him, threaten to report him if he didn't. If I went back to his office, I could record us and then have some proof.

As I watched the rolling hills of the fall countryside pass by my window, nothing seemed familiar. We were way outside of our town. I had no idea where this stalker was taking me. Had I just escaped one predator to be snared by a more dangerous one?

I whispered, "Where are you taking me?"

Xavier's face softened from his glowing rage. He looked at me lovingly, raising our hands from his lap to kiss them. "Home, kitten."

Chapter Six

HOME

"**H**ome" was a cabin in the middle of a dense, green forest. The modern structure consisted of twin two-tiered pods with slightly slanted metal roofs. Full glass hallways connected the pods. The long stone lane crunched as Xavier carefully crawled his expensive car over the pavement.

The house was nestled in a small clearing of trees, perched on a rocky overhang overlooking a calm lake. As we drove up to the cabin, dark blue water peeked between the skinny pines. Rolling down a window, the smell of damp leaves filtered inside the car. The cool air made me shiver. I put up the window. Middle of nowhere, a cabin in the woods, alone with a psychotic stalker—I was in trouble.

Xavier stopped in front of the house on a circular drive. He got out and walked to my side of the car to open the wing. I didn't move.

"Come on. I don't bite." He laughed like a villain at his sarcasm; I knew very well he did bite.

"Can you just take me home, please?" I pleaded, "Please, Xavier."

"You *are* home, Marissa. This is ours or will be ours once we're married. I know you're going to love it. You love the woods." He looked around at the scenery, then said quietly, "I built this for you."

He *built* this for me? His confession filled me with terror. Was he going to lock me inside forever? I'd read news stories like this. I settled back further into the car.

Sensing I wasn't moving, Xavier swiftly reached inside, unbuckled my belt, then grabbed me. He threw my body over his broad shoulder as if I weighed nothing.

"Oh my god, put me down, Xavier!" I hit his back with my fists, and he chuckled.

"You don't have to call me your god, kitten. Master or sir or daddy will do just fine." He spanked me as he walked us along a cedar gangplank across a craggy ravine to the front entry. Black water pooled underneath the walkway surrounding the front of the house; koi fish swam in small clusters through lily pads and lush water plants. The sight quelled me in Xavier's arms.

Xavier placed his finger on a scanner to unlock the front door. "Nah, never mind. I am your god now. I am your savior." He placed me on my feet in the glass entry hall.

My instinct was to turn and run, but I was captivated by the beauty of the cabin. An unobstructed view of the lake filled the back of the entry. I ventured further to my right, where the house opened up. There, I stood in awe of the majestic design.

The tall ceiling was lined with light wood planks, the walls boarded in a darker cedar. However, there was little wall space, given the number of floor-to-ceiling windows. I was standing in a giant, light, and open room complete with a living area, dining area, and kitchen. My nose was filled with the smell of freshly cut timber, reminding me of family camping trips we used to take in the summers of my youth.

The living room boasted the largest limestone fireplace I had ever seen. In front lay a nubby rug, a relaxed soft gray sofa, and an Eames chair with an ottoman (probably the real thing). The kitchen was constructed of smooth wood cabinets, a commercial-sized refrigerator, and a large gas stove. A ten-person rustic wood dining table served as the kitchen's island, the sides flanked with solid benches.

Across the entryway was a sliding cedar door, which I assumed led to a bedroom. There was a metal spiral staircase to the right of the living area leading down to the pods below. The furnishings were sleek but appeared comfortable, dotted with soft textiles. The entire back of the house was glass and held a wooden deck covered with an angled roof, looking over the dark waters beyond.

It was exactly what I would call my dream home. Overwhelmed by the beauty, my eyes glistened with tears. I was so happy a place this magical existed. It did feel like home.

Xavier had come up to stand next to me and

grabbed my hand in his. "You like?" He turned his head slightly to see my reaction.

"Xavier... this is breathtaking. It's a dream."

"Come on. I want to show you out back." He pulled me through the glass doors leading to the deck. I followed willingly, fears subsiding.

There were several natural wood Adirondack chairs in the lounge area and an oversized picnic table in the dining area with a large grill. A hot tub sat by the bedroom quarters. Beneath us was a whole lower level of the house, also backed with glass. Large stones formed a back patio, then converged into a path with stone stairs leading to a dock on the water.

"How many bedrooms are there?" I asked, facing the lake, peering over the modern metal railing. I was curious about this amazing architectural wonder.

Xavier came up behind me, wrapping his arms loosely around my waist and peering above my head into the distance. "Five. Told you if you want a litter..." He pushed his hips and hard erection into my back.

I glanced up at him to see if he was joking or not. He looked down into my face with tenderness and smiled.

"I can't tell if you're serious or not. No one has ever talked to me this way."

"I'm serious, beautiful. Let's get started."

Leaning down to kiss my neck, I inhaled his cedar and spice scent. I should have been terrified he would kidnap and breed me, but my body arched back into him, letting him have more of my neck.

"Xavier... I don't know anything about you. I just

broke up with James. I need time. Mr. Hall, my classes. I'm under a lot of stress. I can't start anything right now." I listed excuses while drifting back into his firm chest, my nipples becoming erect while he sucked on my earlobe.

Xavier kissed down my neck and moved his hands to my shoulders, massaging them. He inhaled deeply. "Mmm, you're adorable."

With a swift motion, he used the hands on my shoulders to twirl me around to face him. He grabbed my neck with one of his large hands, and the other held my hair at the back of my head, tilting it so I had to stare straight into his piercing gaze.

"Marissa, we've already started. There is no going back from this. Ever. Do you understand?" He took my head and nodded it for me. "I own you; you're mine. Do I need to remind you?"

I didn't know what to say.

"Use your words. Do I need to remind you?" I could only open my mouth like a fish. He let go of my neck to slap me in the face. I gasped. He just smacked me… and my pussy flooded. My knees wobbled.

He glanced at my chest, where my nipples had become rock hard. "Looks like you do need the reminder after all."

Xavier ripped the T-shirt I was wearing straight off my body. I tried to back up, but he grabbed my arms. He spun me around, so I faced the metal railing, then locked me against it, pinning my legs between his. Unfastening my purple silk bra, he ripped it down my arms. My large breasts spilled out before he tossed it aside. He reached around and unbuttoned my jeans. I leaned heavily against him, trying to move from the cold, hard railing.

Xavier pulled my jeans down to my knees while holding my arms behind me with one hand. I swayed my hips as the cooler evening air hit my ass. He spanked me hard on my left ass cheek, and tears formed in my eyes. He lowered his zipper.

"You will obey me. When I ask you a question, you will answer, do you understand?" As he said this, he grasped my dark hair with his free hand and yanked my head back so I could look at him.

"Yes."

"Yes, what?" He growled close to my ear.

I thought about this—the titles he wanted me to use. *Keep him calm so I don't get hurt.*

"Yes, sir?"

"Yes, that's right. Good girl." He kneed my legs as far apart as they would go. Then he bent me over the railing, pulled back on my arms with his hands, and rammed into me from behind in one swift movement. "*Fuck!* Let me in, kitten. Don't clench up. Show your owner how much you need his cock."

I whimpered. It never got any easier, that thickness stretching me each time he thrust. I didn't understand myself. I was terrified. He just smacked me across the face, but he was right. My body needed his cock. I milked it with my pussy, fucking him with reverberations every time he pumped into me.

Xavier chuckled under his breath, "That's it. Fuck your cock. It belongs to you as much as this cunt belongs to me." He let go of my arms, grabbed my hair, and pulled back so my neck was stretched up again. "Who does this pussy belong to?"

He was pounding into me so forcefully I could barely get the words out. "You."

"What? I can't hear you." He smacked my face again. "Who?"

"You! You… master!" I was about to lose it. Maybe I was beginning to believe his delusions about me. My body humped his cock feverishly as I pushed with my hands off the rail. I moaned and writhed on it, desperate to have more inside me.

"Damn, you are such a good girl. You want more, huh?" He patted my ass cheek lightly, then grabbed the bulk of it. "Need to get in deeper." He stopped for a moment, reached down, and pulled a leg out of my jeans to hold one of my legs up, knee bent in the crook of his elbow. From this angle, he plunged in and filled me completely. I screamed from pleasure and pain.

He grasped my face with his free hand and looked me in the eyes. "How many babies do you want, Marissa?"

My stomach dropped out of my body, and my pussy clenched hard around his thick cock. "Wha-?"

"How many babies do you want me to put in you?"

Uh… I had no idea how to answer the question without making him angry, but he would rage if I stayed silent. "As… as many as you want, master." The fear took me to the edge, my pussy pulsing in anticipation.

"Mmm, kitten. That's a good answer." He kissed me

71

deeply. His body pressed my hips into the metal so hard I was sure to have bruises.

He began to take some deep thrusts and said, "What if I just want to keep breeding you over and over and over and over?" He punctuated each repeated word with a sharp hip jut, removing his hand from my face to put it around my neck for a steady grip. He started to block my air. My vision became blurry, and my head filled with cotton.

With the thought of being bred like an animal by this erratic man, my cunt clasped his cock, and I came until my vision blackened, little stars appearing before my eyes. He relaxed his hold on my neck just as I climaxed. The world around me came back into view.

His hips pushed into me harshly as he erupted close to my womb. He nuzzled his face into my neck as he did so, still pumping lazily long after he had come.

"Kitten, you are such a good pet. Hopefully, that was baby number one." He dropped my leg and wrapped his arm around me, writhing into me, then murmured, "Gotta get that last drop in there." He pulled me back into his chest, so our bodies were touching everywhere. He tilted my face towards him and latched onto my lips.

The hard pit in my stomach returned. I squirmed, uncomfortable with our intimacy. This maniac had taken me to the woods and said he wanted to give me babies. I had never been more grateful to be on the pill.

I barely knew Xavier, only that he was unpredictable and unstable. I didn't want to get hurt or kidnapped and left here to die. I had to find a way out of this, back to the safety of my home. I broke our kiss, pulling away and shifting my body slightly to get him to slip out.

"Xavier, I… I hardly know you," I said carefully. I didn't want him to get angry with me again.

Xavier narrowed his light blue eyes, and his squared jaw flinched. He yanked up my jeans and tossed me my bra. After adjusting his clothes, he grabbed my hand and pulled me towards a glass door near the end of the deck.

We entered a large bedroom. In the center was a modern bed with a tufted headboard. It was cozy and covered with soft, white linens. There was a thick, white shag rug covering the concrete floor. He pulled me to a wooden dresser and opened a drawer. He handed me a white T-shirt. "Here, sorry about your shirt. I couldn't help myself."

After putting my bra and shirt on, I glanced at him quickly, nervous about what would happen next. He gazed at me in his shirt, lust filling his eyes as he stroked his chin. Was he never satisfied?

"You hungry?" Xavier asked as he sauntered down the hall and back to the kitchen area. I cautiously followed several steps behind him.

"Come on, let's get you something to eat. Sit." He pointed to the dining bench, and I slid in. He opened the fridge and found eggs and bacon there, as well as other supplies. He started to chop up some vegetables on a cutting board he had placed on the table. "Here, chop these, and I'll get started on the bacon."

I took over the chopping, still unsure what was

happening. Was I going to eat eggs and bacon with my stalker? At least I was holding a large chef's knife.

Xavier glanced over his shoulder at me from the large stove, where he was pulling out some pans. "Let's play a game, shall we?"

I didn't know what kind of games madmen played, and I wasn't sure I wanted to find out.

Chapter Seven

A GAME

"Twenty questions. Ask, and I'll answer honestly. Go." Xavier cooked the bacon and gathered my chopped vegetables to fry with the eggs.

Okay… so his game seemed relatively safe. Maybe he wanted me to get to know him. "Really? You'll answer honestly?"

"Yes. That was question one." Xavier continued cooking.

I blew out a breath. "That's not fair."

Xavier didn't look away from the stove. "A fair is what comes around once a year, and you ride rides and eat cotton candy. Next question."

There were so many I wanted to ask. I wanted to delve into my stalker's mind, get inside, see what made him tick. If I did, I could use that information to escape his thrall. Xavier was clever. I could start simple, get him going, then attack with tougher questions. Trap him.

"When's your birthday?"

Xavier snorted while starting on the omelets. "November first. Next."

"How old are you?"

"I'll be twenty-three. Next question."

I huffed. This was less fun than I thought. I could find these answers online. My main question, "Why are you so obsessed with me," seemed out of place. Also quite egotistical.

"What's your major? What are your plans after college?"

"Business. Getting an MBA. Next." He plated the omelets and brought them to the table, then gathered dishes and condiments. I helped set the table while he filled glasses of orange juice, sliding beside me on the bench.

"Will you please expand on your answers? I feel like I'm talking to a robot here," I pleaded and ate my omelet.

"No, that was question six. Next."

"Xavier! Come on…" I guffawed while he was trying hard to contain his smirk. "I suppose you'll run your family's business…" Maybe he'd have to fill them in if I used open questions.

"Tell me about your parents."

"That's not a question."

I sighed. "Do you get along with your parents?"

"Somewhat."

This was not going as well as I had hoped. Oh, my! The omelet and bacon were amazing. I involuntarily moaned as I ate. I was hungry.

"Wow! You can cook. I wouldn't expect that. I

assumed you had butlers and chefs and all that growing up. Did you?"

Xavier paused his eating. "We did." He considered, then said, "But I got tired of relying on them to do things for me. I learned to cook so I could eat whenever or whatever I wanted. I've had pretty bad insomnia since high school, and sometimes I'd fall asleep right after football practice and wake up at three in the morning. I'd go down to the kitchen and cook for myself."

I stared at him, amazed he had given me something of himself.

He took a sip of his juice. "Is that expansive enough for you, beautiful?"

"Yes, thank you. That felt like a conversation."

He ate his food so fast that I had only taken three bites before he slid his plate back and leaned on an elbow to look at me. My stomach flipped at how handsome he was. My cheeks heated.

I took a deep breath and asked, "Um… you played football in high school. Did you have many girlfriends?"

"Yes, I've had a lot of girlfriends, hookups, sex buddies, whatever. No, none of them mattered to me. Not until you." He said this as if it was set in stone, a solid, hard fact. My heart was pounding in my chest.

I looked down so I didn't have to see him answer. I quietly asked, "What's so special about me?"

Xavier inhaled deeply. He looked up as if he had a long answer, didn't want to answer, or was considering how to answer.

He seemed to settle things in his mind and said, "Marissa, I have watched you for a while, and I feel like

77

we are compatible in a lot of ways. I think you love your family as fiercely as I do mine." Xavier pinched some of my hair between two fingers and slid them down a lock. "I think you notice beautiful things, and I appreciate them, too. You're generous and want to give back to the world something meaningful. That is a quality I admire, one I don't possess. You're compassionate to the point you would give up your own comfort and safety." He looked at me pointedly. "To make someone else feel better, be more at ease. And I'm not going to let anyone hurt you." He paused. "Not anymore."

My jaw fell open.

I scrambled for something to say, trying not to allow some unknown emotion overwhelm me. What was it? Awe? Longing? Could I see myself falling for this man? My impulse to touch him was strong, but before I did, he continued.

"And I know we want the same things out of life." He sat up demonstratively and caught my eyes with a sparkle.

I cleared my throat. "A-and what is that?"

"A simple life filled with love, lots of children, large family gatherings, nights spent reading by the fire." He nodded at the fireplace across the room. "And passionate sex." With the last words, he raised his eyebrows up and down.

I could see it. Here, in this house. Creating a home. Stockings hung over the limestone fireplace for the children, playing in the lake on hot summer days. Taking pictures of my family's faces to hang on the walls.

Passionate sex on the deck. He was right. The vision felt like me, like home.

Warmth spread around my body. I always fell too quickly into every relationship I'd been in, but I had never had this kind of physical or emotional reaction to someone before. He confused me. One minute he was smacking me in the face; the next, he was exposing my innermost desires. This was moving too fast, and I was still unsure if he would chain me up in a dark basement underneath the ground somewhere.

He leaned over and brushed his lips against mine while holding my chin. He then pulled me onto his lap.

"What's your next question?" His voice was muffled, his face snuggled into my neck. I was getting wet again and scooted around on his legs.

"Uh…" I was finding it hard to concentrate. "What —what number are we on?"

"Well, *that* is number twelve."

I giggled. He wrapped his arms tighter around me. I asked, "You said you love your family fiercely, but also said you only somewhat get along with your parents."

"Is there a question there?" he asked, leaning to look me in the face.

"Um… care to explain that juxtaposition to me?"

Xavier grinned at my brilliant way of turning that statement into a question. "I love my family fiercely. My father demands a lot of me. We often see things differently, and we end up butting heads often. His wife is kind and good for him, but also annoying with her need to constantly please people that don't matter." He stopped suddenly as if realizing he shouldn't have said something.

"'His wife.' Is she not your mother?"

"No. That's fourteen." Shifting on the bench, he set me down beside him. He gathered our plates and took them to the sink, turning his back to me.

"What happened to your mother?" I saw his strapping muscles tense in his tight, black T-shirt. The tattoos on his neck moved.

"She died." He ran a hand through his hair and gazed out the kitchen window.

I was suddenly growing afraid again but asked anyway. "How?"

"Suicide." He cleaned up the dishes and straightened the kitchen while I watched silently.

"I'm so sorry, Xavier." I could tell he did not want to continue this line of questions. He had grown quiet. I wanted to know more, but would he answer?

"When? When did you lose her?"

"In high school," he answered abruptly, almost as if he were done talking about the subject. I decided to move on.

"Do you have any siblings?" His jaw popped. He turned to me and looked me in the eyes with some emotion, perhaps anger?

"I did," he said with finality, and he leaned back against the kitchen counter, crossing his legs and arms.

I was suddenly terrified to ask the natural next question, but also couldn't resist like watching a horrific accident. "What happened?"

"She was murdered."

I gasped. My mind flooded with questions, but mainly my heart hurt for the young boy who had lost his mother and sister. Was she older or younger? When did it happen? Did they catch the murderer?

Before I could ask anything else, Xavier pushed off the counter, taking a few long strides to the entry hall. "You ready to head back?"

The moon had arisen, and the light streamed through the windows. I needed to get home. I was so tired. It seemed as if I wouldn't have to manipulate my way back. Was he going to let me leave here alive?

"You-you're taking me back home?"

"Yes, and that's twenty. Let's go."

Xavier was quiet on the way home and didn't hold my hand like on the drive to the cabin. He turned on some phonk music, too loud to have a conversation. He raced through the dark, twisted country roads on a mission, speeding through the night to arrive at our destination.

When he pulled up to my university apartment complex, it was already past visitor time, so I knew I couldn't invite him in. Not even sure why I should.

I twisted my fingers in my lap. How would we say goodnight? I didn't have to wait long as Xavier stalked around the car to open my door, hand held out for me to take. He popped the trunk and slid my backpack over my shoulder.

Brushing a piece of my hair behind my ear, he lifted my face and gently tapped his lips to mine. As he pulled back, he breathed on my lips. "Goodnight."

Then he turned, got back into his rocket ship, and flew away.

I stood in the parking lot for a long while, seeing if maybe he would come back and be that overly affectionate man that took me to the cabin, but he didn't. I turned and walked up to my apartment. I didn't understand why I felt so abandoned and why I already missed him.

Kinsley was the only one home, sitting on the couch watching some reality TV show. Sharice was probably practicing her violin or maybe had a concert tonight. Elle was likely with her latest hookup.

Kinsley glanced up when I came in. "Hey."

"Hey." I set my stuff down, grabbed a couple of beers from the fridge, then joined her on the couch, handing her one.

"Where's Xavier?" she asked while staring at the TV and her phone occasionally.

"Uh, who?"

"Xavier, your boyfriend?" She looked over at me, her face serious.

"Xavier Cardell?"

She snorted. "Yes, Xavier Cardell."

Had everyone gone mad? "Xavier is not—he isn't my boyfriend."

She lifted her eyebrows. "Oh. Sorry, he said he was yesterday."

"He said that? When?"

"When he came over yesterday afternoon. Invited him to pizza with us, remember? Told you guys to stop fucking and come have pizza?" She paused and examined me. "Are you feeling okay? You look pale. I mean, I know things with James just ended, but there's no judgment. Xavier said—"

"Xavier said what?" I got that sick feeling in my stomach again.

"He said you two had decided to start seeing each other after James and Jackson. I thought you'd moved on. I figured he was who you and Elle were whispering about last night."

She put her hand on my thigh to get my attention and said, "Hey, like I said, no judgment. James has been a good friend to you. I just didn't see you two being in love, you know?"

I nodded. So Xavier had come here knowing that James was with Jackson that morning. Knowing my friends would let him in my room if he told them we were dating. He hadn't used my balcony; he'd just waltzed right in.

"And you see Xavier and me…"

She looked at me and smiled. "Falling in love, yes." She giggled.

Ugh. First, Elle said we would get married and have babies, and now Kinsley said we would fall in love. I just hooked up with him two days ago! He said he's been stalking me for a while. He read my diaries. After today I did feel closer to knowing a little of the enigma that was Xavier, but I was not ready for anything serious. Serious seemed to be all he understood.

I finished my beer and announced that I was going to bed. Taking a shower helped wash the grime off from the day. After my nightly routine in the bathroom, I changed into a tank top and panties. I settled in bed, hoping I could sleep better than I had the last few nights, but my mind was busy.

James and I had just ended things yesterday. Yes, he truly had been a great "friend," as Kinsley called him. Had I been in love with him? I was not sure. I said the words to him, yes, plenty of times. I loved his personality, his charisma, and his take no shit from anyone attitude. I admired his tenacity and his capacity to love everyone. But did I love him… like romantically?

My mind flashed to the moment Xavier listed all the things about me he thought were special—when he described my dream life. The pull to touch him and feel him deeper inside of me. This nagging impulse to know everything about him. No, I don't think I did love James. Not in a deeply romantic way, I guess. Maybe my friends could see me better than I could see myself.

It was all too sudden. I still had to deal with the possibility of seeing James with Jackson. I wasn't sure how that would affect me, the Mr. Hall situation, my unclear future, and the feeling that Xavier could kidnap, impregnate, then murder me at any time. Hopefully, if I were pregnant, he wouldn't murder me. *That* was a comforting thought.

An innocent Xavier came to my mind, a boy too young to lose his mother to suicide and a sister as well. Growing up with great expectations for his future. I guess he didn't have a choice in where his life would lead. Here I was complaining that I didn't know what would happen with my future, but that was because I had choices.

That was what my painting was about: choices. I had them. Lots of people didn't. I was fortunate to be able to choose where I wanted my future to take me. Knowing I had the choice made me feel more in control.

I was going to report Mr. Hall. If I saw James and Jackson together, it could hurt, but I could handle it. A surge of assuredness overtook me.

I would make decisions about my career and create the life I wanted.

Chapter Eight

CAUGHT

The next day I was fortunate enough not to have a class with Mr. Hall. His course was scheduled for Wednesdays. Instead, I finished my painting throughout the afternoon. Colors gleamed off the canvas as I studied the final product. I was proud of my work for the first time in a long while.

When I woke up that morning, I decided that my semester project would be titled *Choices*, a study of people on the precipice of determining a path. I took my first photo that morning in the rising sun. It was a self-portrait. I stood on an empty road that split in two directions: one leading to the university buildings straight ahead and the other to the woods with a twisting lane that went around the bend of a big oak tree on my right. Lights were sparkling on the asphalt with the dew of the morning. Reviewing the shots, I knew it would be some of my best work.

I ambled towards the university police station, prepared to file my report. Sharice ran over to me, a crowd of students flowing out of the art and music building. Murmurs surrounded the front door where the groups were gathered.

"Oh my god, did you hear?" Sharice was panting and appeared panicked. Her dark skin gleamed with a sheen of sweat.

"Hear what?" I tried to peer over her shoulder.

"They're arresting Mr. Hall. Apparently, he raped a few students. They caught him on camera." The mob parted near the door. Uniformed police officers escorted Mr. Hall across campus, his arms held behind his back. He tried to dip his head and hang his hair into his face.

My stomach knotted. "They—caught him on camera?" *What if I'm on there?*

"Yeah, Ms. Geiser's teaching assistant heard all the gossip." She watched with me as the police marched Mr. Hall into the campus station. "Said someone had been secretly recording him in his studio last year and released the video to the police." She turned to me. "Oh my god. He invited you to his studio. Did he ever…"

I swallowed. If the videos were from his studio, I should be safe. "Yesterday, he got handsy and tried something, but I got away. I was just on my way to… No, I never was in his studio."

Sharice stepped closer to me and reached out her hand to rub my arm gently. "Marissa. I'm so sorry. Are you okay? Why didn't you tell us?"

"I was going to today. I needed to process things." I thought for a moment. "I guess I'll wait and see if the others need my statement or not."

Sharice drew me in for a side hug. "Well, I'm down

if you need someone to go with you. Anytime, really." She then tugged on my shoulder. "You look like you need coffee. Let's go."

As we walked to the campus coffee shop, I wondered who had placed the cameras to record Mr. Hall. Then I worried about who my new advisor would be. Checking my email on my phone, we meandered toward the campus cafe. I had one message from an assistant at the college of arts. He announced that Mr. Hall's class was canceled the next day, but his replacement would be there on Friday. There was a blurb that if you had information you needed to share about Mr. Hall (no mention of arrest or accusations), call a number listed.

Looking up from my phone, I saw Xavier across the courtyard from the art building. He was leaning against the side of the brick wall as if he were watching an outdoor play. His eyes locked on mine, and he smiled astutely. Involuntarily, I beamed brightly. He strolled towards the business building.

Sharice noticed our exchange. "How's that going?"

"How's what?"

She laughed. "Come on, girl." She tapped my shoulder with hers. "I have to live vicariously. That man is smokin' hot."

I didn't want another conversation like the one with Kinsley last night. "I thought you and Ty were… What's happening with Ty?"

"I don't know. Men are stupid. He's all over me, texting me, calling me, then not. Anyway…" We reached the cafe, and I opened the door for her.

We ended up talking about her love life and music

projects for our impromptu coffee date, which was a welcome reprieve from my own worries. I kept the conversation off myself and, most assuredly, off Xavier. It was refreshing to catch up with my friend without feeling the heavy weight of a breakup and having to figure out whatever was happening with my stalker.

As soon as my afternoon classes ended and I made my way home, I called the number listed at the end of the email I received. A woman answered. She was with the city prosecutor's office and took down my information, saying one of the lawyers would be in touch. She offered me a website for an anti-sexual violence advocacy group.

I was in the midst of studying for Art History when Kinsley knocked on my door. "Let's go, loser."

I chuckled and opened the door. "Where are we going?"

"We're heading out to Manny's. Taco Tuesday. Get ready." Sharice and Elle were gathering their stuff in the living room. I quickly changed into a corduroy mini skirt topped with an oversized cropped white sweater and faux suede ankle booties. I found my crossbody purse in a pile of dirty clothes and switched out my necessary items from my backpack. Before leaving the room, I glanced at my nightstand, opened the drawer, and took a birth control pill. I never missed one and may as well be early today than late. Xavier was messing with my mind.

We hiked the mile and a half from campus to the town's center, where Manny's was located on Main Street. It was a popular spot with the college kids on

Tuesdays—half-price margaritas. It was early enough that it wasn't extremely crowded yet, so we snagged a booth in the corner.

By the time we started our second round of drinks, the restaurant was busy, and the bar area was filled with people ordering alcohol and appetizers. The front door swung open, and I inhaled sharply. Jackson Riley stepped in. Trailing behind him was James.

Elle was sitting beside me and put her hand on my thigh. "You okay?"

I nodded and took a swig of my mango margarita. James saw me and smiled shyly. He said something to Jackson, who frowned at me but quickly looked away. Jackson walked towards the bar, and James shuffled over to our table.

"Hey," he said while looking at my friends, but his gaze landed on me.

We all greeted him, then he turned to me and asked, "Hey, you want to go upstairs with me for a moment? I am itching to play darts." I slid out of the booth. James led the way up the stairs to the loft with two dart boards and a pool table. There were doors leading out onto a rooftop patio area that was usually the best place to sit.

James found some darts and handed me three. "Um... I know I walked in with him, but we aren't together. I want you to know that. Nothing has happened since that night, Marissa, I swear." His head dropped, then he inhaled before lining up his throw. He missed badly. "Fuck."

I laughed at his terrible shot. "We are broken up, James. I appreciate the courtesy, though. I do." I took my shot and at least hit the board. "How have you been? I mean, it's only been three days, but I'm used to talking to you every day, you know?"

James' entire body relaxed, "Yes! I know, right? It's been tough not talking to you, just about stupid stuff. I miss that." He threw and hit a single ring. "I know you said you needed to wait for us to hang out as friends, but I do miss you. And I'm not meaning like——" His eyes found Jackson downstairs, standing talking to some football players at a high top. Jackson caught his stare, his face lighting up.

I could see it. Them. Their chemistry. I took a deep breath and let it out. It didn't hurt as bad as I thought it would. "No, no, I understand what you mean." I lined up to take my shot. "You like him." I hit the outer bullseye.

James moved his eyes from Jackson to mine. "What? No, no."

"James, if we're going to try the friend thing, let's be friends. I think I can try—little bits. And friends talk about boys. Jackson, you like him. He's obviously into you."

He threw his dart, and it hit a triple ring. He bit his lip. "I've never been… It's very new. I don't want to use anyone or hurt anyone." He pointed his gaze at me. "Not anymore. I need to figure out what I want, and he knows that."

"But…" I urged him on.

"But… he's willing to wait. And yeah, I think I like him." He checked my face to see if I was hurt.

I nodded, then put on a small smile. "Well, I hope he knows how to waltz at snooty Christmas parties."

James laughed. "Yeah, that's going to be a fun one this year... Can you imagine my mother?"

We both started chuckling and reminiscing about our worst holiday parties at his house with his parents. Laughing with my friend lessened the burden I was carrying. The more we talked, the more at ease I became. I didn't have a future trying to please the stuffy Stevensons, and I didn't have to feel so insecure around James now. That would all be someone else's problem.

Tattooed arms threaded around my waist and jerked me back into a hard chest. "What's going on here?"

James snapped his head and glared at the man behind me. I tried to twist away, but the death grip around me was too strong.

"Um, what are you doing here?" I tried to look at Xavier but couldn't move.

"You flirting with my girl, James? Your boyfriend is right here. Damn, it's true what they say, 'Once a cheater, always a cheater.'"

James launched himself at Xavier, and Xavier slid me to his side. At the same time, Jackson appeared and grabbed James, holding him back. James yelled at Xavier, "Who you talking about cheating, motherfucker? Fuck you, Xavier, fucking *my* girl."

James scrambled to get in Xavier's face while Xavier pushed my body behind his protectively. Jackson tried to wrestle James back downstairs. Xavier chuckled at James' outrage, but his eyes were organizing a massacre. As Jackson wrestled James towards the stairs, James looked at me, his expression filled with pain. "Marissa, are you with him? Are you?"

Before I could even answer, Xavier spoke. "Marissa's with me. She's mine. Stay the fuck away from her. She doesn't need you using her anymore." Then, he seized me into a tight embrace and kissed me. Well, it was more like he claimed my body as his in front of James. He may as well have dropped trow and peed on me.

Struggling with all my might, I was able to jostle him and get a little space between us. I slapped Xavier in the face, leaving a reddened handprint. "What the fuck, Xavier? Who do you think you are?"

Xavier's wrath was directed at me now. "*Who the fuck am I?!* Who am I? I'm your owner. You are mine. When are you going to understand that? I told you to break things off with him, Marissa."

I was about to hit him again and run downstairs to my girls, but he gripped my arm. "Maybe I need to fuck you in front of everyone here, so you get the picture." He pulled me into him and walked my body towards the half wall of the upstairs overlooking the dining area.

"What? Xavier, anyone can see us. Please." Once he moved us to the wall, he started to force my head down.

"On your knees." He pushed harder, so I slid down the wall.

"I'll-I'll suck you in the bathroom, please, Xavier. Not right here." Frantically, I looked around. Anyone could walk in from the patio or come up the stairs. There were also restrooms on this level that anyone could visit.

"No, you'll do it here so they can see you worshiping my cock. On. Your. Knees. I won't say it again."

I have no idea why, but I was soaking my thong as he said the words. Maybe if I were quick enough, I could get him to nut, I'd neatly swallow, and no one would notice. He leaned over me, so it probably appeared from downstairs as if he were leaning against a wall—a king observing his subjects below.

Unzipping his black jeans, I fished out his bulky, semi-hard cock. I stared at his girth for a moment, unsure how I would fit him in my mouth. Relaxing my throat, I licked him, wetting his shaft. I used my hand to feed myself, taking him deeper, slowly stroking with one hand. I breathed through my nose. I used my tongue to circle his top occasionally, then dove back in.

Xavier moaned as I found a good rhythm. I applied more sucking pressure and massaged his balls. As I sucked, I drenched my thighs and reached down to finger myself under my skirt. I loved the control over Xavier's pleasure that I clasped in my hands. I needed him to bust quickly so I could get out of there.

The patio doors opened, and people shuffled inside. I froze with Xavier's cock deep down my throat. He stood still as well. The group was rowdy as they passed us but never noticed what was happening. No one said anything, so I returned to my job.

Xavier pumped his hips into my face, pinning my head against the half wall. Though his moans were louder now, most of his sounds were drowned out by the crowd and restaurant music. He moved one hand from the wall he was leaning over and clutched my hair. He then fucked my face with ferocity. He shoved his cock, thick and hard, all the way down my throat, cutting off my air supply. I panicked, shifting on my knees, trying to get some oxygen.

"Shh, shh. Don't be scared, little kitty. I'll control your breathing for you." Xavier stroked a finger down my face as he said the words, then tugged back slightly so I could take tiny inhales through my nose for a moment before he plunged back in.

Tears trickled from my eyes, and spit slobbered out of my mouth. I was pretty sure I looked a mess, but Xavier continued to fuck my face. With one deep thrust, he pinched my nose and held his cock deep down my throat. I thought I would die, squirming as much as possible to back away from him, my hands clutching his thighs. Just when I almost passed out, he yanked his cock out so I could gulp air through the sides of my mouth.

At the same time, more people entered from the patio. Xavier curved his body around me protectively as slurred words and yells wafted in with the men scuffling beside us. Xavier's lightweight black jacket fell forward as he leaned over me, covering my face. One of the guys, clearly intoxicated, shouted, "Yo! Cardell! Who you got under there? Fuck, can I get in line?"

I couldn't see the man but heard footsteps lumber closer. Xavier growled over his shoulder, "Fuck off. Don't even look at her."

"All right, all right, man… have fun."

As he approached the stairs, the man announced to the group that Xavier was "face fucking some chick." Another man sniggered and said, "Fuck yeah, Cardell!

Make sure she swallows." A cacophony of howls resounded from the group.

Xavier remained still in my mouth as the men walked away. His body covered me as much as he could, standing very close so no one would see me. He waited until they were gone before backing up to look at me.

I was embarrassed, but as I began to feel shame, Xavier said, "Mmm, look at you. So proud to be sucking your master in front of everyone. What a good girl for taking such a big cock down her throat. Showing off what a good slut you are for me." Something about his words made me feel satisfied that I had pleased him, diminishing my indignity.

He tore himself from my mouth and snatched me up by my shoulders. Carrying me bridal style, he marched us a few feet to the nearest bathroom and set me down before locking the door.

I wiped my mouth and caught a glimpse of myself in the mirror. I was a tragedy. My dark brown hair was in knots and tangles, black mascara ran down my olive-skinned face, and my cheeks were smeared with chagrin. Before I could look too long, Xavier was on me. He rammed me into a stall, bent me over the toilet, lifted my skirt, and moved my panties to the side. His cock pounded inside me as he gripped one of my hips for resistance. With his other hand, he held my head down into the toilet. I had to press back, so I didn't end up in the dirty water.

"I have to come inside your pussy. I can't stop. I'm obsessed with coming inside you. Help me, Marissa."

He sounded like a desperate man while he drilled his cock, hard as a lead pipe, deep within me.

The pain of having his cock forcefully shoved down my throat, the fear of not being able to breathe unless he willed it, the humiliation of having those men watching me sucking his cock... it made me almost come. What was wrong with me? All it took was Xavier grinding his fully engulfed dick up and down inside, reaching around to stroke my clit, then spanking my ass hard several times while saying, "Such a fucking nasty girl for sucking cock in front of everyone." *Spank.*

"Dirty girls like you deserve to be fucked into the toilet." *Spank.*

"Ugh... My filthy whore." He spanked me again, and I came.

As he heard me screaming in ecstasy, the sound echoing off the porcelain, he held my head closer to the toilet water and fucked me. Our skin clapped together, the smacks so loud they could probably be heard downstairs. "Whose pussy is this?!" He spanked me with each thrust now, my ass burning in pain.

"Your—yours, master." Each strike was taking away my breath. "I'm yours, Xavier."

When I said this, he unloaded inside me with a loud groan. I continued pushing against the seat with my hands so my head wouldn't land in the water. I was disgusted with the entire night. I was disgusted with myself. Mainly, I was disgusted with Xavier for making me feel this way.

He continued to hump me before extracting himself slowly. I smoothed down my skirt, flipped around, and slapped him in the face. I went to do it again, and he caught my palm. Xavier's icy blue eyes glowered fiercely at me. "You won't see him again."

As he zipped up his jeans, I elbowed him, so he was off balance. Rushing from the bathroom after struggling with the door lock, I could hear him saying something like "stop," but I didn't. I flew downstairs, where my friends were now sitting with some boys, clearly a few margaritas in. I stealthily grabbed my purse. Sharice noticed me and said, "Hey, girl! You been getting some, looks like."

Then all the girls inspected me and started laughing.

"Fuck, he must be amazing... Look at her face." Elle busted out.

A few of the guys standing nearby chuckled, and I wondered if they were the group that saw us upstairs.

I faked a laugh. "Ha. I'm going to head home now. Got to finish that Art History paper," I lied. To avoid the awkward insistences from my friends trying to keep me there, I hustled home before Xavier could find me.

Wednesday morning, I woke up feeling vulnerable from the previous night's degradation. I wanted to avoid campus altogether, fearing that one of the men who may have seen me giving a blow job at Manny's would recognize me. I especially had no interest in meeting Xavier. Fury filled my chest whenever I thought of him.

It was late when I woke up, but I didn't care; I knew I was skipping classes. I texted James an apology for the previous night.

JAMES

Not ur fault

UR not the one who should be apologizing...

R U & Xavier together?

ME

Most definitely not

He left that message on read.

The angry voicemail from my mother was still sitting in my mailbox. After studying, I decided to visit my family to ensure they understood not to allow my stalker in the house anymore. My dad would scare him off, surely. He could spot a bullshitter a mile away.

I decided to escape to my favorite place, the nearby state park, which boasted a natural waterfall. Listening to the falling water, watching birds gather twigs for nests, and observing squirrels hide nuts made me feel better about whatever was going on in my life. At least I didn't have to spend my day gathering twigs and nuts.

I shot landscape photos around the park for the rest of the morning. I knew most of the trails quite well by now. Some hikers allowed me to photograph them for my art project. I was going to need to spend some quality time editing soon.

After lunch at home, I studied for classes. It was almost dinnertime when I finished reading and typing my notes. Putting away my books, I headed to my parents' house. The neighborhood I grew up in was affluent but not pretentious. My parents lived in a McMansion-style house—big, brick, and not my style.

I pulled into our driveway behind my mother's BMW. It appeared Dr. Matlock wasn't finished with work at the hospital yet. He was usually home by dinner but occasionally had to stay late. Maybe I would spend the night since it had been several weeks since I'd stopped by.

When I walked through the front door, I expected my mother to be busy working on her latest sewing project in her craft room. She was obsessed with making accurate historical dresses, particularly from the Edwardian era. The local theater group often recruited her for her dressmaking skills.

"Mom?" I started up the stairs when I heard her voice coming from the kitchen. Heading that way, I slowed my steps when I heard a second voice that sounded familiar.

As I rounded the corner, Xavier Cardell was in my kitchen with my mother, preparing dinner. My stomach did a flip. He stood in the middle of the room, tattoos covered by his white button-down shirt untucked under a gray crew neck sweater, dark jeans, and brown lace-up boots. His sleek black strands were perfectly disarranged. How dare he show up here… especially while looking so good. He noticed me standing in the doorway just as I was about to scream or pull my hair.

"Oh, hey, kitten!" Xavier walked over to me, put one hand loosely around my waist, then placed his lips on my forehead. "We were wondering when you'd get here."

My mother turned around from the stove. She looked like an older version of me with long legs, dark brown hair, light green eyes, and olive skin. She had blessed me with curves and full lips. "Marissa! Finally! It's been weeks!" She continued stirring whatever she was making, and I pulled from Xavier to hug her.

"Hey, Mom. Um… what is he doing here?" Xavier moved back to peeling potatoes.

My mother let out a quick breath. "Don't be rude. We wanted a family dinner with him, remember? Your dad's been dying to meet him. Get the company plates. Set the table for us. Xavier, want to help her?"

"Sure, Mrs. Matlock." My mother gave him a pointed look. "I mean, Mom." He looked over at me and fully smirked as he said this. I was pretty sure steam was blowing out of my ears.

Xavier and I went to the formal dining room next to the kitchen. I stormed over to the hutch to get the company plates. Attempting to whisper, but more like quiet yelling, I asked, "What the fuck are you doing here, Xavier?"

"What do you mean? I was invited, remember? I wanted to meet your family."

"You… you forced me to suck you in front of everyone last night, and now you just show up here as if nothing happened?" I was about to explode. I shoved some plates in his direction, struggling to contain my urge to throw them at him.

Xavier calmly set the table, even going around me to gather some placemats and silverware while I stood like an immovable force. "I showed everyone who you belong to. And now your parents will understand as well." He gathered some glasses from the cabinet and moved them to the table. He paused to look at me and said, "Your father needs to understand that I'm your daddy now."

Shocked, I stood with my hands on my hips, mouth open from the gasp I had just made. I scanned Xavier and pursed my lips, contemplating how to deal with him. He raised his eyebrows to emphasize his last statement, daring me to an unspoken challenge.

Xavier placed some mats on the table and said pleasantly, "Any particular seats you use?"

I didn't even bother to answer. I spun on my heel, then walked into the kitchen to speak with my mother without his audience. She glanced up from the stove at my approach with a sly, crooked smile.

"You didn't tell me how charming Xavier is. And so handsome! What a cutie. He said you and James have been over for a while, and he—"

"Mom, could you not?" I interrupted. "Xavier is not charming. And he's not my—"

"There he is! Thanks for setting the table. Hopefully, Marissa pitched in some." My mom gave me a stern look as Xavier loped back into the kitchen. This was going to be a much tougher tightrope to balance than I had anticipated.

"Meh, she pointed, and I did the heavy lifting, as it should be. Is there anything else I can help with, Mrs.— Mom?"

"No, you have been so helpful, Xavi. I'll finish up. Dad should be home soon."

I looked at Xavier and mouthed, "*Xavi?*" My mother had a nickname for my stalker.

Xavier appeared amused. He took my hand and said, "Wanna show me your room?"

I played along and clasped his hand, digging my nails into his skin. "Sure, honey. Let's go."

On our way upstairs, Xavier twisted my arm around, so my hand loosened from his. He swatted my butt and leaned close to my ear. "Now, now. Be a good girl."

Xavier paused by the family pictures covering the wall as we walked up the stairs. He took a long time to consider each one carefully. He'd ask questions like, "What grade was this?" and "How far did you go in Girl Scouts?" and "You didn't have an awkward phase at all, did you, beautiful?"

He reached an old picture from a family reunion. It was my father, his brother and sister, her husband, my mother, my cousins, and me. My grandparents, my father's parents, sat in the foreground. He pointed directly to my uncle and asked, "Who is this?"

"Um... my uncle." My cheeks flamed and I wanted to change the subject.

Xavier stared at the picture for a long time. He clenched his jaw and then stood back from it. "Were he and your father close then?"

"Uh... I think so. You mean before?" Before that awful day, I still feel some weird childhood guilt about? Before I had to go and ruin my father's and his relationship by telling on my uncle? Making my father sad that his only brother was sent to prison for life?

Xavier asked solemnly, "Or after?"

"Um... no. Not after. I kind of ruined that."

Xavier suddenly grabbed me from the stairstep above him, hauling me into his arms and rushing me upstairs. He knew exactly where my bedroom was and hurried inside, closing the door behind us with his foot. He sat me down on the bed and bent over in front of me until we were eye to eye.

"Ruined what?" He was enraged.

"I-I ruined their relationship? I mean, he only

touched me that one time. He didn't rape me. Not like the others. I got away. Sometimes I think I shouldn't have even—"

"Marissa, please tell me you don't regret saying something. That piece of shit hurt you." He paused to look down and squeezed his eyes shut before staring at me again. His face reddened with emotion. "He may have hurt others." Seeming to gather himself, he gripped the back of my head. "Listen to me. You did a good thing."

I teared up with his intensity, unsure where it was coming from.

"Do you hear me, Marissa? What he did was wrong. You did not ruin them, and he did not ruin you."

I let out a sob. "Stop, Xavier. Please stop." I was ashamed that this man knew such a painful secret from my past, from my family's past.

"You did nothing wrong." He pushed his forehead against mine as I cried. He then gathered me under my arms, holding my body against his, my legs wrapping around his waist. I pushed my face into his neck, trying to stop the tears. His intensity was scaring me.

"You're not ruined. It was not your fault, and you did nothing wrong. Do you get that? How good of a thing you did?" He pulled me back by my hair, so I had to look at him. Kissing each of my cheeks, he gathered the tears with his lips before moving them to mine. I had a sudden urge to deepen our kiss and sucked his mouth with desperation.

Xavier groaned and dropped us onto my bed, his body on top of me, never breaking our kiss. He pumped his jean-covered dick into me, and I bucked against him. We frantically dry-humped one another, kissing as if to steal the air out of the other's lungs. He broke the kiss, put a palm to my face, holding my gaze while we writhed in need against each other. I thought I would come from the heavy weight of his cock against my core.

The hum of the garage door sounded within the room, and I froze. I inhaled and whispered, "My dad!" I pushed Xavier off the bed while he held out his hand for me. We straightened each other's clothes and hair, Xavier adjusting his erection before heading downstairs.

When we arrived, my father was in the kitchen, greeting my mother with a light kiss. His hair was a more golden brown than my mother's and speckled with gray, especially throughout his beard. Appearing older than his forty-five years, he had a constant look of "seen too much" doctors get. He often squinted his eyes with either a genuine smile or as if he were trying to think of an answer to an unknown question.

"Hey, pumpkin!" My dad walked to me as I hurried to hug him.

"Hey, Dad." I broke our hug, then turned to introduce Xavier out of politeness.

"You must be the new boyfriend I've heard good things about. Xavier, right?" Dr. Roger Matlock walked to Xavier and stuck out his hand with a warm smile. My father was tall, about 6'2", but Xavier had a couple of inches on him.

Xavier shook my father's hand and answered, "Yes, sir. A pleasure to meet you. I've heard great things about you. First in your med school class, chief resident in cardiology, beautiful and talented wife and daughter…." He nodded toward my mother and me. "You're a man to be admired." What an ass-kisser. My dad was way too smart to believe this crap.

"Wow, thank you! You seem to have studied up on me." Dad dropped Xavier's hand and crinkled his eyes. Here it comes; he'd cut through Xavier's bullshit, and I would enjoy it immensely. My father put a hand on Xavier's shoulder and gripped him gently. "I like that."

What? Xavier seemed pleased with himself. Dad turned to me, pointing towards Xavier, and said, "I like this guy. Good pick."

I moved my lower jaw forward. "Yeah… he's a good one." I couldn't help but say it with a grimace.

Dinner was ready, and we moved the food into the formal dining room and took our seats. Xavier placed his hand on my thigh. Occasionally he would gently massage it. Every stroke made me wet. I might have left a spot on the chair if I weren't wearing jeans.

"Do you play golf, Xavier?" my dad asked once we all had our food.

"Yes, sir. Member of the Merrick Club. I think I may have seen you there."

"I'm on the course any chance I can get away. What do you normally shoot?" Dad's eyes gleamed. Ugh. Golf talk. My dad would talk for hours with him about this. There was no chance of him not liking Xavier now.

"Oh, usually about an eighty-five. Always working on that swing, though." Xavier made this laughing sound so unlike him that I had to turn my head to see if he was purposefully making a joke I didn't get. My dad chuckled along with him.

I tried quickly to think of something I could say that would lessen Xavier's appeal to my parents. Somehow "Xavier spanked me and called me a dirty whore" didn't seem like appropriate dinner talk. The more I thought about the night before, the feel of Xavier's hand resting on my thigh made me straighten in my seat. Xavier noticed and moved his hand higher while massaging gently.

Fortunately, my mother changed the conversation "Xavi, what do your parents do?"

Xavier stiffened slightly. "My father runs a venture capitalist company. My mother passed when I was in high school. He remarried, and his wife is a party planner."

Mom looked saddened. "Oh, I'm sorry to hear about your mother."

My father interrupted, narrowing his eyes. "Wait… which venture capitalist company? You mean…"

"Cardell Enterprises." Xavier held my father's eyes, then took a bite of his food.

"You're Xavier Cardell. Malcolm's son."

"Yes, sir."

"Huh." My father stared at Xavier curiously for a moment.

I was missing some subtext. The energy at the table was suddenly tense, and I wasn't sure what had changed. My dad's jaw flexed, and Xavier continued to eat. Mom looked back and forth between the two and then at me;

she appeared just as confused as I was. I wanted to lessen the friction.

I cleared my throat. "Xavier is studying business, Dad. He's going to get his MBA after he graduates next semester." My father silently looked at his plate while he ate, but Xavier grinned and squeezed my thigh. I continued, "He's also president of Theta Rho Zeta. They do a lot of charity work for the hospital."

My dad looked up. "That's great. Sounds like you have a bright future ahead of you." He wiped his mouth on his napkin. "We done? Need help cleaning up?"

"Well, I was going to bring out some pie." My mom ruffled her brow.

"Oh, thanks, Suzie, but I'm stuffed. Need to finish some notes." He stood up from the table. "Xavier, it was great to meet you. I apologize for rushing out." He started to walk out of the room towards his office, then stopped to tap on the door frame and said to me, "Pumpkin, come find me before you leave."

That was weird. Xavier seemed wholly unaffected and grabbed another roll from the basket. "These are so good, Mom. Did you make them from scratch?"

Mom tried to ease the tension with a little laugh. "Oh, no. Just store-bought. I enjoy cooking, but baking is not something I have the talent for." She gathered some dishes. "Remember my gingerbread cookies from last year—wait, two years ago?"

"The ones you forgot to add sugar to? Yeah, Mom. I remember." She laughed, and I helped her clear the table for dessert.

"Don't worry, Xavi. The pie is store-bought, too." She moved towards the kitchen.

Xavier finished his roll, then jumped to help us. After pie, Xavier loaded the dishwasher while I washed pans in the sink. Watching this untouchable man load a dishwasher gave me a strange feeling. It was similar to when we were cooking together at the cabin. It didn't seem real.

"Well, I better head out," Xavier said, rubbing his stomach. "Mrs.—Mom, thank you so much for inviting me and for the great meal. I hope to do this more often."

My mom came and wrapped an arm around his waist and pulled him into her side. "You are welcome any time." Then, turning to me with a keen look, she said, "I'd love to do this weekly." I rolled my eyes.

Xavier squeezed her back, then grabbed my hand. "Walk me out?"

I couldn't wait to be alone with Xavier. I never thought I'd feel that way, but I needed to understand what happened at dinner with my dad. We walked outside, and I looked for his rocket ship, but he pulled me across the street to a black and boxy Land Rover. I guess that's why I didn't notice he was here when I showed up.

"This your side piece?" I asked with a smile.

"Ha, yeah. Cheating on the 'rocket ship' with this beauty." He embraced me warmly. He bent his head to kiss me, but I turned my head.

"What happened tonight?"

Xavier narrowed his eyes and raised an eyebrow. "What do you mean? We had a great time, right?"

"I mean with my dad. It seemed... tense at dinner."

Xavier shrugged. "I thought we were getting along well." He pursed his lips. "Didn't notice anything. I'd say our wedding plans will go smoothly." I tried to pull back in his arms to ask him which plans were those, but he wouldn't allow it. He leaned down again and kissed me.

I lost the ability to think with his kiss. One of his hands grasped the back of my head, and one grabbed my ass, pulling me closer. He thrust his hard erection into my belly. I moaned, making him stop kissing and chuckle a breath in my mouth.

"Mmm, night, kitten." He pecked my lips with his one last time, then got into his car and drove away. I stood in the road with my fingers on my lips and clenched my thighs together to relieve some pressure. I was wet. Xavier was a problem. I should not have been lingering after him under the glow of streetlamps, but I was.

I walked back into my parent's house to talk with my father. Maybe he would fill me in on what happened during dinner with Xavier. I found him in his office, typing away at his notes. He squinted his eyes behind his reading glasses and smiled as I entered.

"Hey, pumpkin. Come on in." He finished typing something as I sat in a well-worn leather chair across from his desk. He pushed back from the desk.

"Dad, what happened tonight at dinner? With Xavier?"

My dad sighed and put his hands behind his head to stretch. "Oh, he was a fine boy. I just don't think he's right for you, Marissa." I started to ask why, but he continued, "You know I don't like to meddle. You're an adult, and I can't tell my little girl no. James was a good guy, but I knew he wasn't right for you, either. I think you deserve better, pumpkin. I'm sorry, but I'm your dad. It's how dads think."

"But why? You said you liked him. Then he mentioned his dad's business, and you changed your mind." I sat up more in my chair. "Is it that they're so rich?"

"What? No, not at all. Business is cut-throat, honey. Xavier would spend a lot of time caring for that kind of company. I want my daughter happy, that's all." He was lying about his reasoning; I knew it. However, I didn't understand why he was being dishonest.

I was angry that he would try to deceive me. My dad wasn't a liar, not usually. "Well, Xavier and I are together, so sorry to disappoint. Mom loves him."

My dad smiled. "Your mother loves everyone. It's one reason I love her." He was right. My mom was full of love. She enjoyed giving it away freely. She was naïve and trusting. "You have a bit of her in you." He stood up and came around to hug me.

He sounded tired as he said, "I want you to be careful. Just like when I told you about choosing art for a major, there'd be challenges; I can see some challenges with this boy. I'm not sure Xavier Cardell is the right man for you. You're too good for him." He was trying to look out for me, but why? Was he right?

"Thanks, Dad. I understand." I broke our hug, then walked to the door.

"Don't be such a stranger. Your mom misses you." He moved to sit back down again. "I do, too."

"Love you, Dad. I'll be back soon."

"Love you, pumpkin."

I told my mother goodbye and drove home, giving me time to think. Did I just tell my father that Xavier and I are together? Were we? Xavier certainly seemed to think so. I pondered what my father had said about him. Was Xavier wrong for me? Dad wanted to shield me from something, but I wasn't sure what that something was.

Chapter Ten

FIRST DATE

Oddly, I didn't see Xavier over the next few days. I had grown used to his omniscient presence in my life, so his absence was palpable. I worked long hours in the studio on Thursday, but I kept glancing around campus on breaks to catch a glimpse of him. Friday, I realized I missed having him around. The girls and I went to a club that night, and my skin tingled as if someone were staring at my back while we danced. I scanned the crowd, hoping to see him, but never did. That night, I opened my balcony doors... just to let some fresh air into the stuffy room. He didn't show.

The next morning, I started to worry that something had happened or if I would ever see Xavier again. He had mentioned an "event," but since I had not heard from him, I wondered if he had just forgotten about it. Maybe my dad had gotten to him. Perhaps he felt so uncomfortable after the dinner that he thought I wasn't worth the trouble. He probably used all that marriage and baby-making talk as pickup lines. He took girls to his ritzy cabin to make them wet.

On Saturday afternoon, I decided I had been fooled by a clever philanderer, and as I started to think I'd have to drink the night away, there was a knock on our front door. I was hopeful and ran to it, peering through the peephole, but it wasn't Xavier. I didn't recognize the man in the hall.

"Can I help you?"

"Delivery for Marissa Matlock. Room two-twenty-one?"

I opened the door and took the large box the delivery man held in his arms. I didn't recognize the return address. I thanked him and brought the box to the dining room table. Elle and Kinsley, hearing the commotion, had come into the living area.

"What's that?" Kinsley asked, coming over to look at the box curiously. Elle sat at the table, eating some peanut butter, looking like she had had a rough night and was just now waking up.

"I don't know." I began to open it.

"Who's it from?"

"I don't know, Kinsley."

"Well, open it." She was always impatient.

I got a knife and sliced the box open to reveal a large dress box. Within the tissue paper was an Alexander McQueen dark green satin off-the-shoulder midi dress with ruffles near the bottom. The package also contained a pair of gold leather Louboutin sandals and a Judith Leiber clutch. A note on top of the dress read:

Can't wait to see you out of this dress. -X

Kinsley and Elle were leaning over the box, gasping. "Who sent these?"

Kinsley grabbed the note. "Xavier! Ha! Knew it!"

I grabbed the note back from her, blushing fervently. The girls were looking through the box at the items.

"Married and having his babies. I'm so jealous right now," Elle said.

"Aw, I love you two together! Where are you guys going?" Kinsley said dramatically while putting her hand over her heart.

"Guys, I have no idea what this is about," I said, still confused about what was happening, but so far... I liked it.

"You don't know where he's taking you? That's so romantic!" Elle took her peanut butter over to the couch and flopped down.

Kinsley asked, "Does he have a brother? Or, hell, I'll take a sister? Single dad?"

I grimaced at her mention of a sister, but I laughed. "No single dad, no siblings." It was Xavier's secret to tell or not. I gathered the box and brought it to my room when I received a text notification on my phone.

UNKNOWN

Saw you got the delivery. I'll be there at 7.

ME

Xavier?

Yes, kitten. See you then.

How did you get my number?

I have my ways.

Where are you taking me?

A first date surprise. You'll see.

Hmm, I wondered how he got my number. Maybe from Kinsley? I'd have to ask her later. It was already getting late in the afternoon, and I needed to shower and get dolled up for our date. I was curious how a first date with Xavier would go. What if it was a fancy party at his parents? Memories of events at the Stevensons flooded my mind, and I cringed.

After eating some simple food for dinner, Kinsley and Elle helped me get dressed for the evening. I wore a nude lacy strapless bra and matching panties underneath the dress. I sprayed on my favorite perfume and packed the little evening bag. I was touching up my lipstick when he arrived at the front door. Kinsley went to answer it, and I heard her gush over how handsome he looked. My head was spinning.

I stepped into the living room, and there he was. I took a deep breath and walked towards him. I tried not to swoon like a Victorian lady, but Xavier looked glorious in his custom, tailored brown suit, crisp white shirt, and dark green patterned tie. He even had a paisley pocket square.

Xavier turned from greeting my friends, holding a large bouquet of red roses. When he saw me, his eyes turned up at the corners. He opened his mouth into a smile but grabbed his jaw and chin, stroking them appreciatively.

"Damn, beautiful. I did good." He took a few strides to stand next to me, handed me the bouquet, and pressed his lips against my cheek. "You're stunning."

"You clean up well," I said to him, smirking.

"I'll take these for you!" Elle said, grabbing the bouquet. The girls were pretending not to gawk at us. She started to put the flowers in a vase, filling it with water, but her eyes never left our interaction. Kinsley gave up pretending to be into her book and decided to take our picture for us.

Before she did, Xavier pulled out a small velvet box from his pants' pocket. "I didn't want these to get lost in the package."

I opened it to reveal gold hoop earrings. "Wow! Xavier, this is all too much. I can't thank you enough."

"You just did by allowing me to look at you."

I took out my earrings and put the new pair in. After our first couple's photo, Xavier took my hand and led me to the door, wishing my friends a good night. We reached his rocket and took off to our unknown destination.

Xavier wasn't giving any hints as to our destination, even when I was poking his side while he was driving. He giggled at one point and then told me not to tell anyone he did that. He held my hand so I wouldn't tickle him again.

"It seems you know my roommate, Elle."

"Yep. We went to grade school and middle school

together. Hadn't seen her since she showed up on campus her freshman year."

I tried not to be insecure with Xavier, but I still didn't know what kind of playboy I was dealing with. "Oh? She mentioned you asked about me."

Xavier snorted. "I'm sure she did."

"Did you guys know each other well?"

"Marissa, are you asking if I slept with smelly Ellie? The answer is no."

I punched his arm lightly. "Hey! Why'd you call her that?"

He laughed. "Just a stupid school-age prank."

We pulled up in front of a glass building I didn't recognize, but it had a sign above that said, "Artayo Gallery." Were we going to an art show? Gallery opening? Xavier *got* me. This is precisely the kind of date I'd want to go on.

We parked in the lot, and he opened my door, helping me out. As we walked inside, we were greeted by a woman holding a tray of champagne. I took one, but Xavier passed. He walked me into the showroom, my hand clutching his hard bicep.

"What is this place?" I asked.

Xavier smiled and kept leading us toward a room in the back of the gallery, passing other artists. "Our company invested in this place recently. Thought you may enjoy the opening." He nodded to an elegant older lady with white hair dressed in a ruffled black jumpsuit. "The owner, Lorraine Michele."

Lorraine stepped up to us with a gentle smile. "Welcome, welcome. This must be Marissa Matlock. People are asking about you."

"I'm sorry?" I was confused. Who would ask about me?

Lorraine looked at Xavier, and she smiled again. "Enjoy the show," she said, then glided away. I peered up at Xavier, but he wasn't giving anything away and continued to lead us on.

When we arrived in the back room, my heart skipped at a collection of portraits lining the walls. I teared up in embarrassment, confusion, and gratitude. My pictures, my works, were here, in this gallery.

"Xavier... did you?" I had to take a breath, "Did you do this?"

Xavier reached down and said, "I hope you like it," against my temple before kissing there.

"Where did you... Did you force poor Lorraine to...?" People were viewing my photographs. My pictures were in a gallery. "You shouldn't have made her put them up like that."

"I didn't. I showed her some of your work from the basement at your parents' house; your mom showed them to me. Lorraine loved them and said she wanted to show them." Xavier held up a hand to show off the portraits. "This is all you, Marissa."

I was holding back my tears, trying not to ruin my makeup. "Thank you, Xavier. No one has ever... This was so kind."

"Kind? No, your work needs to be seen. You're an incredible artist and photographer. I'm privileged to get to view it." Xavier took a finger and stroked it over my cheek, gathering a tear.

The rest of the evening, I talked with patrons, Lorraine, and curious viewers about my work, discussed the projects displayed in the other areas of the gallery, and introduced myself to a few artists there. Xavier was around, but he mainly stood in the background while I answered questions. He brought me hors d'oeuvres and drinks when needed and even held my bag for me as I talked.

"So, did I do good for a first date?" Xavier asked when we reached his car at the end of the event.

I pressed myself into his body, pushing him against his car, reached my hands around his neck, and pulled him in for a deep kiss. "Perfect, Mr. Cardell." I felt intoxicated on bliss.

"Mmm, not perfect, yet. I have to take you out of this dress." He placed his lips on my neck and sucked, giving me goosebumps down my arms and back. "Your place or mine?" he whispered.

I hadn't been to his place since Red Night a week before. Maybe creating new memories in that room would help me to get past the bad ones. I knew my roommates would be way too nosy to let me live down the screams I intended to make. "Yours," I said breathily as he continued to nip and suckle on my neck.

We arrived at the manor in record time, Xavier placing my hand on his hard dick throughout the ride while I gently stroked it. He would moan and say, "Hmm, kitten, that's too much. You're going to make me come in my pants."

He drove into a garage that looked like a converted horse stable and jumped out quickly, hustling over to get me out of the car. As he tried pulling me by the hand towards the house, I pleaded with him to slow down. I couldn't run in my expensive heels. He looked at them, threw me over his shoulder, and ran into the house. I laughed at his enthusiasm.

Once inside, I heard Xavier say, "Not now, busy," to some brothers, then rushed us upstairs. He threw me on his bed and climbed on top, loosening his tie and throwing off his jacket. I was undoing his belt and trying to unzip his pants. "Get up. Turn around," he ordered.

He unzipped my dress and let it fall to the ground. I slipped out of my bra and panties and ditched the shoes while he got naked. He ogled my body. Licking his lips, he said, "Be a good pet and ride me, kitten."

Xavier pulled me into his body and crawled to the bed. He propped his head slightly on a stack of pillows, and I leaned over him, breasts dangling in front of his face. He took them in his hands and rubbed his head between them. I started sliding up and down his shaft, getting it wet with my juice.

I leaned forward and pushed his dick inside my entrance; I was going to take it slow this time. As I leaned back and down onto his thick cock, we studied each other's faces while our bodies fully connected. Xavier tried to force his eyes open as he groaned in plea-sure. I let my head drop back and began to ride rhyth-mically, enjoying every single inch of his thickness. I squeezed him with my thighs and sat up to hop lightly on his lap, ending with a flick of my hips.

"That's it, kitten. You look incredible." Xavier grabbed my breasts with his hands, rolling my nipples around, and pinched them. I arched my back to push my breasts out further. He let go of one to grab my ass with his other hand. He massaged there, then spanked me. "Ride this dick. Damn, your pussy is so wet and warm." He spanked me again.

I leaned over him to bounce harder on his cock, moving my hips up and down quickly. As I did, my breasts landed in his face. He began to suckle my nipples, then bit down hard. I screamed.

"Mmm, that's it, feed me. I'm a growing boy." He sucked harder, swirling his tongue around each. I started to writhe forcefully on his cock. Twisting my gathered hair in one hand, he pulled my head back and continued to grab and spank my ass with his other hand. He stuck one of his fingers in my mouth. I sucked, and he moaned. He grabbed my ass, then slid the wet finger inside it. I gasped at the pleasure of it.

"Fuck, Marissa. I don't want to cum yet." He shut his eyes tightly. "Fuck, you're gonna make me cum. This pussy is too good." He groaned and jabbed harder into me as I pushed down onto him. I sat down hard, ground into him, and my internal muscles clamped down for a long, hard squeeze. I screamed his name while at the same time, he yelled, "*Fuck*! I'm coming…"

I could feel his cock pulsating with the last of his ejaculation while my pussy throbbed around him erratically. I kept moving with gentle writhes, draining it. I wrapped my arms around his neck, and we kissed, breathing heavily into each other's mouths while he still spilled inside me.

Xavier rolled me over, so he was on top but stayed inside me. Our bodies were tangled together, legs intertwined, his hands in my hair and mine his. He gazed into my eyes. "Marissa, you're amazing; I never expected..." He kissed me before completing the sentence. "You made me come too quick, beautiful."

Xavier punched me inside with his semi-hard dick and said, "Give me a few, and we're going again." I bit my lip and nodded emphatically.

We fucked all night. At one point, he ordered pizza, and we ate on his bed, talking about nothing in particular in a dazed-out sex high. We fucked in his shower, on the desk, and in the window seat as he kept moving us around. He said he wanted to cover every surface with my body.

By the time the sun was coming up, we were spooning, exhausted. Xavier was still pumping his cock inside me, though I was pretty sure he was half asleep, if not fully. He woke up enough to rub my clit, forcing me to come for the innumerable time that evening while he came with a hoarse grunt. Then, he kissed the back of my neck and pulled me closer. Finally, he fell back to sleep, still buried inside my pussy.

Feeling his soothing warm breaths on my ear and his hard body fully entwined with mine, I fell asleep.

Chapter Eleven

BLISS

The next several weeks were filled with Xavier. Usually, we slept in his room at the manor. He would fuck me awake every morning. We would eat breakfast, and then he would go to the gym before class. It inspired me to hike more often in my favorite park, taking pictures along the way.

"Where's Elle?" I asked Sharice as we found our way to the section of the cafeteria that was now "ours." I started to choose a chair next to Xavier, but he slid my food tray in front of him and snatched my waist, so I plopped down on his lap.

"I don't know. She's been absent recently. And I mean secretive. She always has been, but now it's worse, you know? I've seen her come and go from the apartment, but she hasn't shown up for lunch. Maybe we should check in with her." Sharice was cozying up to a Theta Rho Zeta named Maurice. He grabbed her attention from our conversation with a whisper in her ear, which caused her to giggle.

"Who are you talking about?" Xavier wrapped his arm around me and spoke into my ear softly.

"Elle. She's been noticeably gone from social functions."

"Maybe she's just doing her own thing. I wouldn't worry too much." He brushed back my hair as I started to cut my salad.

"Did you already eat?" I asked, spearing a tomato with my fork.

"Not what I wanted."

"Oh?" I knew what he was implying.

Xavier spoke into the back of my neck, his lips brushing my skin and causing goosebumps to spread down my arms. "Yeah, need that pussy in my mouth soon, or I'll starve."

I laughed. "You ate it this morning for breakfast."

"That was *hours* ago." Gripping me tighter, he pulled me up higher on his lap, adjusting me so that I could feel his erection in his pants. His appetite was insatiable.

"Hey, Cardell. Marissa, where's your friend?" We were interrupted momentarily by another few TRZ brothers setting their lunch trays down. As the weeks progressed, our section had become like the "popular kids'" table in a high school cafeteria. My roommates and I often hung out with the fraternity, but Elle had been noticeably absent recently, while Sharice and Kinsley had made more appearances than normal.

"Which friend?" I asked Caleb, a tall, thin guy with short brown hair.

"Your hot one, what's her name? The blonde." Behind me, I saw Xavier shake his head at Caleb, who was sitting two brothers down and across from us. "Oh. Nevermind."

Furrowing my brow, I turned to Xavier. "What was that?"

He answered with a little kiss on my lips. "Eat. You gotta get to your next class. Let's go." Swatting the side of my butt, he emphasized his point. Xavier was right. I needed to head to my photography class, which I enjoyed now that I wasn't sexually harassed.

Xavier would meet me after my last class in the afternoons. He would take us to the library or his manor to study and sometimes to my art studio to work. Then we would meet friends someplace for dinner. We would spend every night together except on Wednesdays.

On Wednesdays, we would cook family dinner with my mom, but Xavier would leave for fraternity business meetings. It was our one night apart from each other. My dad suddenly had cardiology society meetings, poker night, or was on call those evenings. I hoped my father's absence didn't slight my boyfriend. If Xavier was upset, he stayed silent.

Sundays were pizza and wine nights alone with my girls, but Xavier would sneak into my room through the fire escape and wait in my bed until I returned. Tuesdays, the "popular kids" would all head to Manny's and take over a corner downstairs by pushing several tables together. I noticed Kinsley getting cozy with a certain TRZ named George, or "Big G," as everyone called him, and Sharice was definitely over Tyson. Fridays, we would all head to the only night club in town.

Saturdays were reserved for Xavier and me. We

would head to our cabin in the woods and enjoy the crisp fall air. Xavier took us out on the boat a few times. I would bundle in blankets until we'd find a quiet spot. He showed me how to fish once, but most often, he would cast while I would catch the last of the autumn sun before the winter cold set in. Painting on the shore or photographing nature around our house became my coveted weekend activities—I was living my dream life.

Xavier was an amazingly attentive boyfriend. He supported my work, studying for his classes while I painted, sculpted, or edited photos in the little studio. He and Sharice accompanied me to the prosecutor's office when I left my statement about Mr. Hall. The lawyers did not think I would be needed in court, so my videoed deposition seemed to be the end of it for me. I was relieved.

Ms. Savitri, my new advisor, was vastly different from Mr. Hall. She helped me gain insight into my work and myself. Our advising sessions turned into therapy sessions, which motivated me to expand my artistic abilities. I was excited to showcase *Choices* at the end of the year. Gretchen, as she asked me to call her, said my work was "a subtle whirl on common themes," "sparkling in its use of natural light," and "raw with fresh emotionalism." She offered explicit methods to improve my pictures.

A few days before the big TRZ Halloween party, Xavier and I were catching up on our studies in the library. Bored, I watched the crowds of students preparing for mid-terms. Scanning the large study hall, I saw the redhead from Red Night a few tables over glaring at me. I checked behind me to make sure it was indeed me she was looking at. When I turned back around, she got up and made her way to our table.

Xavier was scanning his book (he *was* an incredibly fast reader) and typing up his paper. The redhead slinked next to him and ran her finger along his arm to get his attention. He barely glanced at her before saying, "What do you want, Caitlyn?"

"Hey, handsome. Just wondering what your costume is for the party. I wanted to match like last year." Caitlyn looked like she might try to sit in his lap if he wasn't so close to the table. I wanted to rip her arm off of his. Were they going to the party together?

Still staring at his book, Xavier said, "Go away, Caitlyn."

Caitlyn glowered at me. Leaning over, leaving nothing to the imagination with her low-cut sweater and skin-tight jeans, she said close to Xavier's ear, "I thought we could still have a few romps before you mate… or even after."

Xavier moved his eyes across the table where George was sitting. Big G got up from his seat, took two strides over to Caitlyn, and grabbed her arm.

"Fine, fine," Caitlyn said. "I'm leaving. See you later." She blew a kiss at my boyfriend as Big G led her away down the aisle of tables.

I closed my open mouth. My boyfriend continued to speed-read as if nothing had happened. "Um, what was that about," I asked him.

"Something not worth talking about."

"Well, it certainly looked like something to talk about to me. Who is she?"

"No one." He still didn't look at me.

"She didn't seem to think she was no one. Are you going to the party with her?"

Xavier exhaled and said, "No. I'm going to the party with you."

"I don't know… maybe you're not," I said and crossed my arms. I was livid with his non-answers.

He finally put his book down and turned to me. "Are you jealous, kitten? Cause I kind of love that," he said.

"I'm not jealous. You're just being evasive."

Xavier placed an arm around my shoulders, and his other rested on the table in front of me, trapping me. He brought our heads close together and said, "Okay, fine. Ask me. What do you want to know? Have I fucked Caitlyn? Yes, many times. Am I currently fucking her? No, I'm loyal to my girl. Did I ever have feelings for her? Fuck, no. She's a conceited, manipulative bitch."

"Oh," I said. "When did you last…"

He shook his head, "I don't know, probably over the summer. She was a warm hole and a willing masochist. That's it. Can I get back to my book now?"

I pondered what he told me as he returned to his book. I couldn't concentrate on studying now. What if Xavier needed multiple people like James did? Did he want to fuck her, too?

"Who were those two blondes you were with before?"

He sighed. "Kara and Brooke. Yes, I fucked them,

too, a few times, actually. Together. Do you want more detail?"

"Are you bisexual?"

Xavier snorted and shook his head. "No. Definitely straight," he said with amusement. He adjusted his hoodie and sat up straighter, preparing for an interrogation.

"But you and James…"

"I fucked an ass. I like fucking asses; they're tight holes to fuck. Do I fantasize about men, am I attracted to men? No."

"You've never fucked my ass…" I said it with a pout.

He reached over to massage my neck, "Believe me, that's coming. Especially after this conversation."

"How many men have you been with?"

"Two: one, I fucked while high on E, and his girl sucked me off after." He paused, then said, "The other, the night I was holding you when I fucked that asshole. I did it to show you what he was, that he wanted something different than you. I knew he wasn't what you needed."

He gave up on his book and pushed back from the table, then pulled me onto his lap. He whispered in my ear, "You deserve to be the *only* in someone's life. I'm not interested in Caitlyn. I'm not interested in men. I'm not interested in anyone else. Just you, Marissa. *Only* you." I pushed into him as he kissed my neck, feeling his growing hardness.

"Mmm, you keep doing that, and I'm going to be interested in you right now," he said.

I smirked before giving him a mini-lap dance. I

could feel his cock jump at me through his joggers. Xavier reached down between us, causing me to lift a little.

"I guess my kitten needs her cream," he purred in my ear. He gathered up the back of my loose mid-length floral skirt, pushed my panties to the side, and moaned when he felt my wetness. I felt him pull down his sweat-pants while I hovered above him. We both glanced around before he guided me onto his waiting cock. He arranged my skirt around us, so no one would see what was happening.

"Now, I need to study. Don't move." Xavier reached his arms around my waist and returned to his book, occasionally typing on his laptop.

What was he expecting me to do? Just sit on his cock? I could feel it throbbing inside me and tried to shift, but that made things worse as he thickened within me. Lips dripping with wetness, my clit was hot with need. I writhed to feel him, my head dropping back to his shoulder.

Xavier took one hand, grazed it under my sweater and bra to find my nipple, and clamped down on it. My pussy pulsed around his dick, and I almost yelled. His mouth covered my ear. "I said, do not move."

I stilled on his lap, worried the other students nearby would catch what was happening under the table. Everyone was busy with their work; if they noticed, no one bothered to look. Big G came around the corner, lumbering towards our table. He was a large human, standing probably 6'5" and 300 pounds. His dirty blonde hair reached his shoulders and was usually held back in a ponytail. He rarely spoke, but when he did, you could feel the reverberations in his deep voice.

"Xavier, G is coming back." I started to stand up.

He pushed me back down. "So?"

"Xavier, he could *see* us!" I whispered.

"And?"

"And I really don't want Kinsley's, um… guy, to watch us. It's weird."

Xavier kept reading and answered, "So don't move."

How could I stay still when all my body wanted was to grind on the big cock in my pussy? It was impossible to concentrate on my studies. My nipples begged to be sucked, clit angry it wasn't being rubbed.

With his free hand, Xavier lifted the front of my skirt, sliding his palm slowly up my inner thigh. He spread my folds with two fingers and began to tap my nub with the pad of his middle finger. I almost peaked, but the fear of having an orgasm in front of a room of people kept me from losing control. It was torture.

Big G sat down. He glanced at us, then said to Xavier, "Taken care of." He began typing on his computer, which looked like a child's toy underneath his hands.

The finger tapped harder on my clit, now adding a second. I wiggled my hips and tried not to whimper. To stop the breathy pants from becoming too noticeable, I leaned back and turned my head into Xavier's tattooed neck. My legs dropped to either side of his. From this angle, Xavier could pump his dick in a few inches and pull back. With this new sensation, I couldn't contain my moan any longer.

Big G didn't even look up. He sighed pointedly and then firmly shut his laptop. He quickly gathered his stuff and left. I barely heeded his exit as the fingers clicked faster, drumming my clit rhythmically. Xavier jacked his dick inside me.

"You need to come, beautiful?"

I nodded into his neck, sucking a little there so I wouldn't cry out.

"Beg me."

I would do anything to come but was afraid to speak, fearing I would scream if I opened my mouth. I sucked harder on his neck.

"Beg me." Xavier removed his fingers from my clit and hit my open pussy with his palm. "Beg me." He hit it again, soft enough not to make a loud sound but firm enough that I bucked.

I whispered, "Please, please, master, please... please... daddy, let me come." I was delirious.

"You're a disobedient girl. You wouldn't stay still, and you deserve punishment." He spanked my pussy again. I was going to come anyway if he kept doing that.

"I'll be good, I promise, I'll be good. Please let me come, master."

His fingers went back to tapping gently on my clit; his dick slowed its pump. "You'll be obedient? You'll do as I say?"

"Yes, yes, I'll do exactly what you say. Please, master." In this position, I had no control over my own pleasure; I was at the mercy of Xavier's benevolence.

"Mmm, you're so compliant. Look at you with your brain turned off, allowing your daddy to fuck you in front of all these people. Such a good girl." He rubbed on my clit hard with several fingers and thrust quickly again. I was going to come.

Xavier's head was turned slightly towards me as I snuggled against his neck. He said, "Shh, shh. Don't think. You don't need to keep thoughts in your pretty head. I'll think for both of us. Just be compliant and obedient. Come for me. I'll allow it."

Writhing harder, I bit his neck and pushed forward on his fingers as he held them down on my clit, cock pushing up into me as much as he could. My body jerked, legs trembled on either side of his. I came all over him, feeling the wetness gush onto his lap.

"Good girl." Xavier moved my hips back and forth roughly on his crotch. He stopped breathing as he worked me, then let out a sigh of relief as he came. He pressed his lips to mine and said, "I think we just made a big mess." I chuckled, feeling the puddle we were sitting in. I was enjoying my afterglow, putty in his arms.

We straightened up, gathered our stuff, and left the library before anyone could report us. The good thing about being Xavier Cardell's girlfriend? No one would dare.

Chapter Twelve

HALLOWEEN

The TRZ Halloween party was the best party of the year. It seemed as if the entire university had been invited. The fraternity turned their guest cottages into haunted houses, each with a different theme. As guests arrived, they would make their way through the houses in sequence. The last was designed as an asylum escape room. If you escaped, you would be carted to the big party filling the downstairs of the manor.

Most drinking games were held inside as the colder autumn air prevented people from venturing too far out on the back patio. Two beer pong tables were set up in the dining room for a lively competition, complete with judges and announcers calling out the shots. Kegs were lined up in the reception area just to the right of the entryway, with long lines of partiers waiting to fill their cups. The furniture had been pushed against the walls in the larger games room, where a DJ booth was set up with an impromptu dance floor. Costumed revelers were doing funnel shots near the bar there.

Kinsley and I were in the kitchen, taking themed liquor shots with Xavier and his friends. Elle and Sharice were elsewhere in the sea of roisterers. Arriving earlier that evening, I dressed like a sexy lion in a romper with a maned hood while Xavier was my tamer in his ringmaster suit with a leather whip. He had even grown a black handlebar mustache for the role.

Though I had seen them on campus and in the house, I learned more about Xavier while observing him with his three closest friends. Big George Turner and he had been tight since high school, where they played football together. Levi Joseph was his childhood pal whose father worked as Cardell Enterprises' chief financial officer. Mason Locke was his cousin. Very few people had insight into the depths of Xavier. These men were his inner circle, and I wanted to glean all their knowledge.

Kinsley and I finished our conversation as we heard Levi say, "Dude, you missed like three opportunities. Go back to the range."

Mason huffed and said, "My gun locked up; what did you expect me to do?"

Xavier answered mockingly, "'My gun locked up.' Locke, find another excuse for once."

"Oh! Oh, this coming from the guy who couldn't hit that sharpshooter five feet in front of him. Marissa, you actually let this guy put his dick in you?" Mason, dressed as Batman, turned to me, making a gagging sound.

The boys had played an airsoft match earlier in the day and were heated about the loss. Big G was standing next to Kinsley; the two dressed as Han Solo and Princess Leia. She giggled at the boys' ribbing.

Levi said, "Speaking of... *Fuck*, I need some pussy. Kinsley, you busy right now?" He ran a hand through his wavy light brown hair and showed her his panty-dropping half-grin. Kinsley laughed and glanced at Big G, who grunted and stared at Levi blankly. "Fine, fine. I've pissed off the big guy. Can't compete with that horse cock anyway."

Levi poured another round of shots. He was dressed like a sexy fireman with suspenders and no shirt. His body filled out the costume well.

"Who's your other friend, Marissa? The tall blonde," Mason asked.

Xavier laughed and said, "Man, you'd probably miss all her holes anyway. Why're you asking?" Mason glared at him.

At the same time, I asked, "Who? Elle?"

"Yeah. Elle." Mason said her name slowly, his intoxication becoming apparent.

"Dude, that girl's been around. I wouldn't bother." Levi passed out the drinks, then looked at Kinsley and me before saying, "No offense."

Xavier punched him in the arm. "You're one to talk, Levi."

Mason jumped in, "You're both a couple of whores. G, remember that party in high school when they both fucked that one chick and her mother at the same time?" Mason laughed. "Lev, didn't you end up screwing her mom for a while after? Or wait, was that Xav?" The room seemed to be getting tense, but Mason didn't notice.

"Locke, shut the fuck up," Levi said.

"Ha, then her dad walked in. Fuck, I still don't know how you're alive—"

"Shut the fuck up, Locke," Levi said again.

"What? What did I say?" Mason looked around the room.

Big G lumbered out of the kitchen, and Kinsley followed. Xavier slapped Mason on the back of the head. "You fucking moron."

Levi yelled, "What the fuck, Mason? We told you not to bring that shit up."

"What am I missing?" I asked quietly.

"Oh, shit, guys. I'm sorry. I forgot." Mason took a shot. "I'm getting in the hot tub." He walked out of the kitchen.

I eyed Levi and Xavier, who exchanged a meaningful glance with each other. Levi took his shot, then walked out behind Mason. Xavier took his drink and kissed me on the forehead.

"Want to head upstairs," He asked, purring in my ear.

"What was that?"

"What was what?"

"Come on, '*Xav*,' don't play. You fucked someone's mom?"

Xavier sighed and said, "Lev fucked G's stepsister for a while in high school. G didn't know. His dad's wife of the moment liked to get dicked down by both of us, Lev and me."

I took a shot. "Oh."

"G walked in on us all fucking at a party once, and we try not to mention it now. I kept fucking his stepmom after she and G's dad divorced. I had just lost my mom. She was nice."

"Oh. I see. How long did you…" Did they have a relationship?

He seemed to cut to the point of my question and said, "Marissa, I never cared about anyone until you. I told you that."

I put my arms around his neck and kissed him. He tasted like our candied apple liquor shots.

"So… upstairs?" he asked, pushing his body into mine.

"No, come on. We're going to dance. It's a party."

Xavier held one of my hands to his crotch. "Well, there's a better one right here in my pants."

I snorted and pulled him from the kitchen to the games room. The strobe lights and fog machines created an appropriately eerie atmosphere. The DJ was playing remixes of popular spooky-themed songs, the bass causing my chest to beat harder. Given that it was a TRZ party, plenty of couples were openly fucking in the middle of the room while calling it "dancing."

Xavier grabbed my waist and spun me around. My back was flush against his chest. I pushed my ass into his crotch and started to grind on him, snaking an arm around his neck. Swaying with me, he held me close, so our hips never parted. We continued our dance for a few songs, getting hotter with each one played, his erection continuously stabbing my lower back. Wanting to torture him a little longer, I dropped down and slowly wiggled up his body.

"Someone's getting fucked in the ass tonight," he said close to my ear. Then he spanked me.

"I'm ready," I said, and he snatched my hand to lead me upstairs as if he had been waiting for me to say the words.

Big G was near the wall holding Kinsley by the ass while her legs were around his waist. She was so small compared to him; I supposed it was the only way they could face each other. They looked deep in a heated conversation. Xavier tugged my arm. I'd have to ask her about it later.

As we passed the hall bathroom, the door wasn't shut all the way, and Levi was leaning back on the sink, pants around his ankles. He was holding his cell phone, videoing a girl sucking his cock. The door blocked my view of who it was.

We reached Xavier's room, and he pushed me forward with a little shove. "Crawl to the end of the bed."

I dropped gracefully to my knees before slinking across the floor. Knowing Xavier was watching, I swiveled my hips, wanting to give him a good show. Halfway to the bed, a sharp snap of pain landed across my backside. I yelled and stopped.

"My little lion needs her ass tamed," Xavier said behind me. "Keep crawling."

I approached the bed on my knees. Xavier whipped me again. I jerked and screamed.

"Have you been fucked in the ass before?"

I shook my head, and he whipped my ass again. I sobbed.

"What was that? I couldn't hear you."

"No, sir."

"Mmm, I love virgin ass. Stand up and undress. Everything off." As I did, Xavier went to his closet and returned with a flat metal bar and other items. "Lay on your stomach on the bed." Pussy dripping with anticipation of the unknown, I did as I was told.

Xavier bent my legs up and out to my sides, leapfrog style. He strapped my ankles to the metal bar that held my legs apart. He then grabbed each arm and pulled them underneath my body, so I had to lay my head to the side. Each wrist he strapped into cuffs attached to the bar. This naturally made my hips rise, exposing my core. He walked to the side where my face was lying and put a red rubber ball in my mouth.

"Bite down." Xavier tied the gag around my head.

Worried about what would happen next, I heard a crack in the air and my thighs quaked. Another sharp bite landed on my ass from the whip. I cried into the gag.

"You're going to be a good girl for me. Let me fuck you hard in the ass." He whipped me again. I was sure to have marks.

Xavier stopped, and I heard a bottle of liquid being squeezed, some drizzling onto my backside. "This is an appetizer." Pressure built on my forbidden hole as he pushed a plug inside. He went slow, twisting, pulling in and out, getting me used to the feeling. I moaned. James toyed with plugs in my ass before, so I quickly got used to the sensation. When it was finally all in, my body relaxed with pleasure.

"Look how wet you are. Fuck, you love this. This is why we're so good together, kitten." With the sting of the whip I cried tears of satisfaction. He was right. With James, I didn't know what I wanted; he wasn't right for me or what I needed. He hindered my ability to explore my fantasies. Xavier opened a new world for me, exposing my innermost desires.

I craved his control over my pleasures, and I savored the pain.

At his last whip, my legs trembled. I was desperate to be fucked. Xavier bent behind me and licked my wet folds. I arched into him as much as possible and whimpered in my gag.

I heard Xavier undressing, then the mattress dipped as he knelt behind me. He turned the plug a few times while situating himself just at the edge of my entrance. Xavier inhaled deeply and said, "I can smell you. You need to be fucked." His big cock suddenly filled my pussy, thrusting harshly into me, smacking my reddened ass and thighs. There was no way I could resist with the bar spreading me wide open for him. I worried about what his thick cock would do to my little asshole.

"So obedient. So compliant. I bet you'd let me do anything to you. You'd do anything I told you to do." I whimpered and nodded. When his dick was inside me like this, I would.

The plug was suddenly pulled from my ass, and more lube drizzled into my gaping hole. Xavier pulled out and replaced himself with a vibrating rabbit-style dildo. It was not as big as Xavier, and I missed the feel of him. His dick edged the entrance of my back hole. He started to push inside slowly, but I flinched. He smacked my ass.

"Relax, relax. Open up. Let your master control your body. Submit your ass to this cock," he said while pushing in further as I focused on trying to relax my muscles. I tensed up again with the pain of how big he was, crying out into my gag. Xavier turned up the vibration on my clit, and my body loosened with pleasure. "There you go."

He seated himself fully in my ass and groaned with deep pleasure. "Fuck! Fuck I don't want to come yet. You are so tight. Fuck, gonna come deep in your ass. Hold still. Don't move."

All I wanted was for him to move. It wasn't painful, just uncomfortable. Xavier let out a breath and began to fuck my ass, dragging himself out, then slamming back in. He picked up the pace, pulling my thighs back into him each time he'd bang my backdoor. His hand came down with a hard slap on my ass, already hot from the whip. I jolted from the pain, my insides recoiling.

"Ugh, it feels so good when you do that." He spanked me again, harder. I sobbed and involuntarily squeezed my pussy around the dildo, ass around his cock. I was so full I didn't even have time to think about it; I came quickly, screaming into the ball gag.

"Oh, fuck, Marissa. That's so tight I can't... you're strangling my dick. I won't be able to pull out of your ass... Guess my cock lives here now."

I wanted the vibrator off of my clit; it was too sensitive. He continued to slap my ass over and over again, plunging into my hole, not caring that I was trying to escape the pressure.

"You are such a dirty girl. Taking a big cock in your ass while tied up. Dirty slut. You're my slut, my little fuck toy now." Xavier was enjoying working my ass. When he spanked me again, I came a second time. My clit was too sore; I wanted to wiggle the dildo out but couldn't move. I whimpered into my gag.

"I'm gonna cum in your ass. You'll love it. Sluts love cum in their assholes." Xavier's cock began to pulse, and I knew he was about to explode. He shoved his dick all the way to his pubic bone, filling my anal cavity; the gag muted my scream. As I felt hot ropes of cum spray inside my ass, I came again all over the dildo, sliding back onto Xavier to get him even deeper inside me.

Xavier yelled, "Fuck, fuck, fuck!" He left his cock in my ass for a moment, then pulled out with a pop. His cum dribbled down to my pussy. "I've owned all your holes now, kitten. I own all of you."

The restraints began to feel uncomfortable, and Xavier quickly released me from the binds, then removed the dildo and my gag. I collapsed onto the red velvet comforter as he walked to the bathroom and turned on the water. His body slid next to mine on the bed, and he put his arms around me, gently kissing my neck and back, caressing and massaging my thighs and butt.

He said softly, "Go get cleaned up, and I'll join you in a bit."

Walking felt funny. All our juices flowed between my

legs as I stood. I was glad for a little private time to clean up before getting into the hot bath. It was a large claw-foot tub. Settling into the bubbles, I rested my head against the cold porcelain until Xavier got in behind me.

Moving my hair out of the way, he massaged my shoulders as I leaned my head against his chest. The hot water soothed my sore pussy and ass. Xavier took a washcloth and gently washed my body with his soap. It smelled like him, rustic and manly. I was almost asleep when he sat up and stepped out of the tub. He dried us off and wrapped a robe around me and a towel around his waist.

When we reached the bedroom, a charcuterie board filled with delicacies was lying in the middle of the bed. The side tables held glasses of water. We ate, and he told me about a costume "malfunction" he witnessed from one of the brothers downstairs. I almost choked with laughter on my cheese and crackers, and he had to pour more water from the carafe.

I shed the robe, and he the towel. We slid under his silky sheets. I snuggled against his chest, one leg thrown over his. Before I fell deeply asleep, he kissed my fore-head and said, "I love you."

I was suddenly wide awake; I wasn't sure if I had truly heard him or dreamed it. I lifted my head from his chest, and he was staring into my eyes. Clearly, he said, "I love you."

My eyes watered. "I love you, too, Xavier."

His face softened as he kissed me and breathed into my mouth, "Say it again."

"I love you, Xavier." This was the first time I had been in love.

He moaned, and I settled back on his chest, listening to his heart beating a steady rhythm. As I was about to fall asleep again, I heard him whisper, "I love you, Marissa. Goodnight."

Chapter Thirteen

THANKSGIVING

Autumn breezes were changing into winter winds as the Thanksgiving holiday approached. My love and I were planning to split the time between our families. My mom, dad, and I usually spent the lunch hour with my father's sister and her family. Then my parents and I would visit my mom's family, where her brother and sisters (all three) and their respective families would have a huge gathering.

Xavier explained that his holidays were usually skippable with just his father and his father's wife, Millie. Since high school, he and Big G would go to his aunt and uncle's to spend time with Mason. Levi would usually come over after his family dinner, and they'd all get stoned and watch football together. This year, however, we would start a new tradition. We'd visit his family for lunch and mine for dinner.

I was nervous about meeting Mr. Malcolm Cardell and his wife and went through several outfits to find something to wear. I settled on a wide-checked tan turtleneck sweater dress that reached just above my knees. It was form-fitting but not clingy. I paired it with faux suede boots and my brown satchel bag. I curled, then fluffed my long hair into a low ponytail.

The big Land Rover picked me up from my apartment. Xavier jumped out, and my heart raced. Dashing in his slim-fit coffee-colored turtleneck and gray striped pants, he quickly reached the passenger door in brown crocodile boots. His aviator sunglasses were on so I couldn't see his eyes, but he smiled as he saw me and said, "Fuck… kitten. You look amazing. Do we have time to go back upstairs?"

After slapping his arm, I laughed and said, "No, but definitely later. Let's go." We headed off to his house.

Well, "house" was a misnomer. Georgian in style and stately in nature, the red brick mansion stood behind a short stone fence with a long, paved driveway curling towards the entry. The front door had been decorated with a wheat wreath and gigantic planters filled with mums of all colors. Smoke spilled from each of the four chimneys atop the roof. Large bay windows flanked the front, while dark green shuttered windows lined the rest of the house.

"You grew up *here*?"

"Home sweet home." Xavier stopped the car in front of the door.

As we entered the parqueted entry, a robust woman with ruddy cheeks and gray hair approached, grabbing Xavier in a hug. "Xavi, so glad you came here this year. I made all your favorites. And no sweet potatoes near your seat." Taking a gander at me, she exclaimed, "Oh, my. This must be Marissa."

The woman warmly embraced me and said, "I'm so thrilled to meet you. You are beautiful, just like he said. I'm Charlene, but call me Mama C. I take care of the cooking and cleaning when I feel like it." She broke the hug to stand back, thumbed towards Xavier, and laughed. "And cover this one's messes." I instantly loved her. "You want any secrets on this man, I'll tell you."

"Marissa, don't believe a thing she tells you. Her memory has been failing these last few years, and she likes to make stuff up." Xavier smiled as he marched us toward a formal living room to our right.

A tall man that could only be Xavier's father jumped from a floral sofa where he'd been reading a book. He took off a pair of wire-rimmed glasses and smiled brightly as he saw us. He had the same icy-blue eyes, black hair, and chiseled jaw as Xavier. His father, however, had a few days old beard and gray sprinkled on his temples. He was strikingly handsome.

Like Mama C, Malcolm hugged his son tightly, then broke the hug with a sharp pat on his back. He said, "I missed you. So glad you decided to come." He was casually dressed in a navy cable-knit sweater and chinos; wool-lined moccasins covered his feet. Maybe I had overdressed.

Xavier was holding my hand. He said, "Dad, this is Marissa, my girlfriend. Marissa, this is my father, Malcolm Cardell."

"Marissa, wow. I am so glad to meet you finally. Please just call me 'Mal.'" He took my hand and shook it heartily. "I don't know if you're a hugger, but you'll probably get one from me after a couple of drinks. And definitely from my wife." He paused, then yelled, "Millie! They're here!" His eyes gleamed as he gave me a big smile.

A petite, gorgeous blonde woman entered dressed smartly in a turquoise cowl neck sweater with matching wool pants. She wore dangly pearl earrings and was barefoot, displaying perfectly painted red toenails. "Oh, Marissa! I couldn't wait to meet you!" Mal was right. His wife ran straight to me and hugged me snugly. Her head barely made it to my chin. "I'm Millie. We are just so excited for Xavier to bring you home, *finally*. Sorry, Xavi," she said as she turned to Xavier. "Missed you, buddy." She then hugged him.

"Missed you, too, Mill."

A family of huggers. Xavier was affectionate, so I guessed that's where he learned the trait.

"You guys hungry? C made all your favorites, Xavi. Marissa, I hope you like pie. We didn't know what kind, so we made a bunch of different ones. Let's see. There's pumpkin, pecan, chocolate, coconut, lemon…" She led us through the kitchen and into a formal dining room, listing off all the pies they had baked. I was overwhelmed.

Mal walked behind me and gently rubbed my shoulders with his hands. "Just play along. She's been so excited since we knew you were coming."

We sat down at the formal dining table, traditional in style. We were served by Mama C course after course of delectable foods, each a modern twist on an old favorite. Xavier had his own dish of mashed potatoes and stuffing, apparently made just how he liked, and no one else was allowed to eat it.

"Xavier showed me some of your portraits, Marissa. Millie and I went to Artayo gallery to view more of your work. You have incredible talent. Really impressive," Mal said. Millie was nodding next to him enthusiastically.

"Thank you," I responded. Then to Xavier, I quietly said, "You showed them?"

He nodded, "Of course. They were curious."

Millie smiled at me and said, "Heard you loved the cabin décor. I helped Xavi with it. I'm very proud of how it turned out. He showed me your Pinterest when we were finishing it for inspiration."

So that's how he knew... Pinterest. Xavier shoveled some mashed potatoes into his mouth.

"Yes, I love it. It feels like home."

Millie said, "So when are you guys planning to move in there? Before or after the wedding?"

I coughed and choked on my turkey, then drank some water while Xavier patted me on the back. I regained some control and asked her, "The wedding?"

Mal addressed me, "Oh, by the way, Marissa. Please tell your father not to think about paying for a thing. Unless you think that would be an insult. Maybe I should call him. Xavier, should I talk with him about it? Would you mind giving me his number? Oh, but your parents are coming to our Christmas party, right? I could ask then, I suppose."

"Christmas party?" I looked over at Xavier, who

continued to stuff his face with food. "I'm sorry, I don't…" I floundered, looking to my boyfriend for help.

Millie interrupted, "Oh, no. Was it a surprise? Xavi, did we ruin it?" She slapped her hand over her mouth.

Xavier swallowed. "No. They're coming. Probably best to wait and ask him then." Xavier grabbed my hand on the table and pulled it into his lap.

Millie sighed in relief and said, "Thank god. I thought I messed up there. Well, Marissa, I certainly want us to sit down with your mom and discuss venues, themes, you know, all the fun stuff! Unless you want to go on your own or hire someone, there's really no pressure. I just love to do it. I never had children, so Xavi is like mine, and you'll be my daughter." Her eyes glistened, and she wiped them with her napkin. "I'm so sorry. I am just so happy you're joining our little family."

Mal reached over and put his arm around her shoulder. "*We* are, Marissa. We are so very happy you'll be a part of us. It feels… more complete now. Especially once you guys have your first child." Mal lowered his head towards Xavier as he said the last part.

Xavier heaped stuffing with gravy in his mouth. I was lost in a bizarro world. I didn't want to be rude by asking more questions; it may seem like I was rejecting their kindness. Recalling my experiences with the Stevensons, I had expected coldness, trying to win the approval of rich, snobbish royalty that didn't know how to love. Instead, I was co-starring in a *Donna Reed Show* episode. Somehow my life had been planned, and I was already married and pregnant with Xavier's baby.

Until Xavier and I could discuss things in private, I

would pretend to be the dream daughter-in-law they desired. I looked at Xavier's family and said, "You two have been so welcoming, and I appreciate the warmth you've shown me. I feel like a part of the family." Xavier squeezed my hand on his lap.

After dinner, we lounged in their TV room, the men watching football. Millie discussed wedding plan options, going over different "themes" and "color stories" I could choose for the spring wedding I was apparently having.

As we waved our goodbyes and headed to the SUV, I jumped in and stared at Xavier in astonishment. Xavier turned on Christmas music and drove off toward my aunt's house. I waited for him to say something, but he started singing along to the tune.

Finally, I burst. "What the hell, Xavier?!"

Unphased by my exclamation, he answered, "Hmm? *It's beginning to look a lot like…*"

"Seriously, Xavier. Stop." I turned off the music. "What the hell was that about?" I didn't know my voice pitch could reach that high.

"What was what about? They all loved you. I knew they would."

"I just spent an hour making my wedding plans with Millie for a wedding I didn't even know I was having."

"Oh, yeah. She loves doing it, but if you don't want her help, she'll understand," Xavier said, keeping his eyes on the road.

"Xavier," I said to see if he'd look at me. "Xavier. I don't remember you asking me to marry you. We have only been together a few months."

Finally, he glanced at me and picked up my hand. He said, "Well, sometimes you just know." He kissed our interlaced fingers.

"But… I *don't* know. I mean, I can see a future with you, but I need more time to *date* you." I was worried he'd be angry.

"Okay. Got it. Love you." He focused on the road and smiled briefly.

"Okay. Great. I love you, too." I settled back in the seat. Huh. I guess I had won that argument. He could tell his over-loving parents to back off. Maybe we could discuss something other than wedding plans and babies next time.

We reached my aunt's house, and the kids were playing in the yard with the leaves. After introducing Xavier to my extended family, I hugged my parents hello. Xavier and my father shook hands but didn't say much to each other. Xavier sat with my dad, uncles, and older cousins, watching football in the TV room. My aunts, mom, and I were in the kitchen sharing wine.

My aunts gushed over how attractive Xavier was, how nice, how rich, smart… My mom's youngest sister tried to pry into how big his penis was, but my mom yelled at her. I raised my eyebrows and gave her a knowing look, and she laughed. "He's a keeper, then!" she said.

It was almost dinner time, and I went to find Xavier so we didn't get stuck at the kid's table. He was not in the TV room with the other guys. Neither was my father. I glanced outside, but I didn't see him there. As I passed the den, I noticed the door stood slightly ajar. My father was sternly addressing someone and stood back to listen.

"So, what, you're trying to hurt my daughter to get at me?"

Xavier responded, "Things have changed for me. You know what you did—"

"Look, I didn't know. I swear I didn't. If I could go back…" There was a pause. "Just leave her out of this. Break it off sooner rather than later. She doesn't deserve to be hurt."

"Not happening."

"You—"

"Marissa! I missed you!" My little cousin, Chloe, found me eavesdropping in the hall.

"Marissa?" my father said inside the den. Busted.

The door to the den opened, revealing my father and Xavier. Both had ruddy faces and tense shoulders. My father was squinting. I smiled brightly. "Dinner's ready!"

"Thanks, pumpkin." My dad brushed past me.

Xavier came out behind him and kissed my cheek. My cousin made "ooh" noises at us as we walked into the dining room, hand in hand.

After dinner, I couldn't wait to be alone with Xavier.

"What happened in there?" I asked as I buckled my seatbelt.

"It was a good meal, I thought. I liked your uncle Ken. He was funny."

He was avoiding my question again. "Xavier, what happened in the den with my father?"

Xavier flipped on some music that filled the small

space, making it more difficult to converse. He wasn't rude, however, and replied, "Oh, just a minor disagreement. That's what in-laws do, right? Disagree with you?" He smiled at me briefly.

"What was the disagreement about?"

"What? Sorry, can't hear." I flipped off the stereo.

"Xavier. Seriously, what was the disagreement about? I didn't think you two talked much."

Xavier focused on the road for quite some time before responding, "We don't."

"So then why—"

"Marissa, drop it. It was nothing." He stated it definitively.

Irked, I sulked into my seat. What was going on between the two? Their heated exchange didn't seem like "nothing" to me. Neither did the tension at their first meeting. And why was my father avoiding Xavier? I knew Xavier had closed the subject; my father wasn't giving up any answers, either. I'd have to discover them on my own.

Recently, we had been alternating whose place we were staying at, so I assumed he'd come upstairs with me after he dropped me off. He helped me alight from the car, and his arms embraced me. He gazed into my eyes and kissed me deeply. We stood in the parking lot this way for several minutes in silence. When he pulled away, my body shivered from his lack of warmth.

Xavier quietly said, "I love you. Goodnight." Then he got back in his car and drove away.

I was left standing there confused and a little scared. His goodnight sounded more like goodbye.

Chapter Fourteen

CHRISTMAS

It was the last two weeks before finals, and I had not seen Xavier. Whenever I would text him or call, he was either "busy studying," "tied up with fraternity stuff," or "helping my father." He would always end the reply with "I love you."

When I drove to the Theta Rho Zeta manor, I was told Xavier wasn't at home by the guard at the gate. He usually let me in without question. Now, it felt like I was a stranger in my own home. I texted Xavier as to his whereabouts.

X

Sorry, working with Dad at the office.

ME

Will I get to see you later?

I have to study for that econ final.

I miss you.

ILY

The rest of the week, I spent time finishing up my photography project for the semester. I was finally satisfied with my work, and so was Gretchen. The collection was featured in the halls outside our art studio. Several professors made positive comments underneath the most prominent piece, my self-portrait.

> *"Outstanding look at what's within."* [Gretchen
> had left this comment.]

> *"Lightness fooling us with its brilliance; darkness
> undermining in shadows beneath. Excellent
> work."*

> *"This was no* Choice. *This was assuredness
> of a well-performed project."*

A buyer from the gallery had approached Lorraine. One of my portraits sold for enough to allow me to buy some expensive lenses I had been eyeing. I was ecstatic, but the guard at the TRZ station said Xavier wasn't there when I visited to tell him. When I called, his voicemail answered. I texted him instead.

ME

Hey, there was a buyer for one of my portraits from the gallery.

Are you coming to family dinner tonight?

X

That's amazing, kitten. Can't. Helping
Levi. Sry. ILY

Dejectedly, I went home to tell my parents my good news. My father's car wasn't in the drive as I pulled in. When I told her, my mother hugged me and said she knew I'd be a famous artist from the very first picture I took with my disposable camera in third grade.

"Thanks, Mom."

"Well, I'm going to buy a cake right now so we can celebrate tonight. Is Xavier coming?"

"No, he couldn't make it. Finals."

"He is so dedicated. He's going to make such a great CEO of that company." She walked to the mudroom to get her purse. "Oh, by the way, Marissa. I received the Cardell's holiday party invitation. We are really stepping up in the world," she joked. "Millie Cardell herself called me to invite us, too!"

"Oh, that was nice. How'd she get your number?"

"Guess Xavi gave it to her."

"Xavi has your number?" I reluctantly used my mother's pet name for him.

"Yes, figured if you two are this serious, I'd need to get in touch with you sometimes. Anyway, Millie seems so nice. We discussed you two. Both of us are excited to see what your future holds." Her face lit up with expectation.

"Yeah. We'll see." Lately, it didn't seem like we had much of a future together. Xavier hadn't let me out of his sight since we first hooked up on Red Night. Now, he was fading faster from my life than my dark-washed jeans.

I finished the chicken casserole my mother had prepared and slid it into the oven. There were green beans in the refrigerator, and I set them aside to cook as a side dish. Taking my time and trying to avoid thinking about my doomed love life, I got out the flour and started making half-hour dinner rolls. Keeping my hands busy helped keep my mind calm.

When my father arrived home, my mother was still gone. He kissed my temple while I rolled the dough balls, placing them in a pan to bake. I pointed to a towel, and he handed it to me so I could wipe my hands.

"Hey! You came for family dinner!"

"So what's this about your portrait? It sold from the gallery?" My parents visited the art gallery when my collection was displayed a few months ago. I told my dad about the sale. "I am so proud of you. Where's Xavier? He not coming tonight?"

My father and Xavier hadn't talked (that I knew of) since Thanksgiving. "No, he's busy tonight… I actually came to talk with you about something."

"Sure, pumpkin. What's up?"

"Dad, I have to know; please be honest with me. What happened with Xavier? Thanksgiving, the night you met… something is going on with you two."

My father looked down. "As I said, I don't think he's the right man for you."

"Dad, please. There is something else going on! Xavier's avoiding me. You're avoiding looking at me." I pleaded at him with my eyes. "Dad, I *love* him. He hasn't been around, and I miss him. Xavier's going to be in my life. I want you to get along."

"Maybe it's best that you haven't been spending as much time together." He sighed.

"You're really not going to tell me." Anger flushed my face. "Fine, I'll figure it out myself." I walked out of the kitchen towards the stairs. My father told me to wait, but I ran up the stairs to my old bedroom and locked the door.

Xavier must have found something in my old diaries, something he and my father had in common. It seemed to have to do with my father and me. Xavier had asked Elle about my father's name a few years ago. I had to find their connection.

The journals were labeled by school grade and sparsely filled with entries. I was terrible about keeping up with them through the years. The only entries were when I had overwhelming emotions I needed to deal with. It had been easy for Xavier to pick out significant events in my life.

Just as I settled in to re-read my diaries, my mother yelled from the kitchen, letting me know that the cake was ready. Descending the stairs, the family reunion picture caught my eye. I remembered Xavier's intense reaction after seeing it. Did it have something to do with my uncle? My father's brother? It was a lead I would look into.

Unfortunately, it was another week before I could research further. I had exams to study for, art projects to finish, and Elle hosting semester-end parties in our apartment, bringing over a new boyfriend that no one liked. Sharice practiced her violin concerto for her semester-end performance in her room, filling our apartment with the sounds of missed notes and discordant tones. Kinsley was going insane with the stress over her finals and would storm about slamming doors and cabinets. I tried to quell tension within the apartment when I wasn't actively studying.

Xavier had maintained his distance from me for another week. I missed having sex with him but longed for our nightly cuddles and how much he made me laugh daily with his snarky comments. In the back of my mind, I formed dark scenarios that he was with another woman or planning to end things with me, but didn't know how to let me go.

After my final exam on Thursday afternoon, I texted him, but he had a fraternity meeting and was helping his family prepare for their weekend event: "*ILY.*"

When the Cardell holiday party arrived, excitement flooded me unexpectedly for an event I had dreaded. I couldn't wait to be able to spend the whole evening with my boyfriend. Two weeks was too long for me to go without gazing upon his handsome face. I was too embarrassed to tell him how often I stared at our pictures on my phone or stalked his social media accounts.

Xavier sent me another gown. This one was made of gold sequins that hugged my figure. I paired it with my gifted heels and purse. A local jeweler crafted a classy pair of monogrammed cufflinks for Xavier; I planned to present him with the gift that evening. The box just fit into my tiny evening bag.

Waiting for Xavier, I sat at my little bedroom desk, careful not to muss myself, and pulled out my laptop. Using a search engine, I started investigating my uncle's crimes. Details and all names were sealed in court records due to the victims' ages. There were no photographs except my uncle's crazy mugshot.

When I searched Xavier's name, I could only find that his sister, Olivia Cardell, had tragically died in the local hospital after a serious "accident" at age eleven. There were no details about what kind of accident it was. Olivia had been born the same year as I was. She even looked like me with dark hair and olive skin, though her eyes were blue like her brother's.

Lucia Cardell, Xavier's mother, had also died in an "accident," but at home. The articles listed Xavier as age fifteen at the time of her death. A black-and-white photo of a father and son grieving at her funeral was shown along with the news story.

Xavier arrived at the apartment, and I rushed to meet him after two weeks apart. I lost my breath at the sight of him in a custom black tuxedo. His eyes sparkled as he saw me. He crossed the distance between us in two glides and embraced me, devouring my lips. We stood in the living room, enjoying each other for a moment while Sharice sneaked back to her room from the kitchen.

"You're the most beautiful woman in the world. I've missed you," he breathed into my mouth with his eyes closed.

"I missed you so much. I love you. I can't get over how good you look," I replied.

He kissed me and grabbed me into a tight embrace

before pulling back and guiding us to his Land Rover downstairs. After all the Stevensons' parties, I was nervous about what embarrassing situation I might find myself in. I imagined Mal pointing out other, more appropriate young women for his son to set his eye on. Millie may ignore me in favor of those more important. At least my friends and family would be there if I needed solace.

The Cardell holiday party was an illustrious event in our quaint little town. Millie obsessively planned for it all year. As Xavier and I arrived at the Georgian mansion, we were treated to a spectacular lights display and fully lit blue spruces lining the path towards the house. Faux snow machines blew crystal flakes in glittering arcs across the drive on our approach.

We were greeted by valet staff and directed around the side entrance of the house by a path of candy canes entwined with white lights. Guests milled slowly to the main event held in a large clear heated tent on the back lawn. The smell of pine made me nostalgic for Christmas mornings past.

Near the tent, the pool had been transformed into a full skating rink with adults and children swirling around the ice. The attached gazebo area held a glowing firepit with couples cozied nearby, sipping mugs of steamy liquids. A few children were making snowmen out of the fake snow.

Inside the tent, red-clothed tables circled a center dance floor. A red throne was located at the far end of the room, and Santa Claus sat greeting a line of children. Oversized red, green, and gold ornaments of all shapes and sizes hung from the ceiling. The walls were lined with giant glowing candy canes. A gigantic tree glowed with warm candlelight and was surrounded by large, wrapped gifts in colors matching the other decorations.

Everyone who was anyone was in attendance, including the mayor. Local celebrities, artists, and businessmen were gathered in small groups, networking and enjoying served cocktails. It was a formal event with ball gowns, sequined dresses, and tuxedos flourishing throughout the house and grounds.

I found my parents near our assigned table at the head of the room, and Xavier led us over to greet them. The Cardells were standing nearby. My roommates mingled with some of the TRZ brothers and Xavier's friends one table away. Malcolm and Millie generously invited my extended family, and my cousins were standing in line to tell the big guy in the red suit what they wanted for Christmas.

"I can't get over how magical this place is, Millie. Again, thank you so much for your invitation." My mother was speaking with the Cardells.

"Oh, no, thank *you*," Millie responded. "We both couldn't wait to meet you. I hope you enjoy the food. I hired a new caterer this year and I'm eager to see how everything tastes."

As we approached, my father shook Xavier's hand,

then turned away to sip his scotch. Millie grabbed me for a side hug. Xavier kissed my mother's hand, and we were welcomed to the party. Mal was distracted, speaking with some of his associates, so I didn't have a chance to say hello. I wondered how our parents' introduction had gone.

"Well, you're welcome to our place anytime. Xavier's been coming over for family dinner on Wednesdays. We love having him."

"Oh, we adore your daughter. She's been such a joy in our lives these last few months." Millie smiled at me as she said so, and I grinned back.

Yes, his parents had been overwhelming, but I'd learned to accept their excitement just like Xavier had received my mother's. Maybe our families weren't too dissimilar. Fears of the ghosts from Stevenson's parties past left me for good. If these types of events were in my future, I'd welcome them.

Mal tapped a glass with his fork to get everyone's attention. "Please, everyone, please take your seats. It is time for the first course." Everyone started moving to their assigned tables. My parents were assigned seats next to the Cardells. My mother leaned over to whisper in my ear, "Told you. We *have* moved up the social ladder. Maybe they heard about my baking."

I giggled. "I doubt that, Mom." Xavier sat between his father and me, rubbing my cold hand to get it warm. Millie was on the other side of Malcolm. My parents were on my right.

My father sipped his glass of scotch and flagged down a waitress for another. He never drank more than two, but tonight he seemed nervous, squinting his eyes more than usual.

"Dad, you okay?"

Dad forced a smile and looked away, sipping a new scotch.

Malcolm stood at the head of the room and rang a small bell. People glanced up from their conversations. Mr. Cardell's booming boss voice resonated through the tent. "Before we begin, we have an announcement. Xavier—"

Xavier swallowed, setting his face as if he was off to confront a dragon. He squeezed my hand and led me to the middle of the dance floor as the room turned their heads to watch. I tried not to trip on my gown and concentrated on the floor. I felt as if I were being led to the gallows. What had once been a boisterous event suddenly transformed into a silent affair. All the stares from the massive crowd penetrated my skin like daggers.

In the middle of the dance floor, Xavier spun suddenly and dropped to one knee. There was an audible gasp from everyone, including me. The room was rotating slowly before my eyes. My brain couldn't understand what was happening. Xavier pulled a ring from a velvet box in his pocket and held it to my finger.

"These last few months with you have felt like a lifetime, but an eternity with you could never be enough for me. Marissa Matlock, I love you with every piece of my being. I'm obsessed with you. Will you do me the honor of becoming my wife?"

Anger and embarrassment hit me like a freight train. Instead of giving him an answer, I considered running away. I could go somewhere no one knew me. I had already told Xavier it was too soon to get engaged just a few weeks ago, yet he was proposing in front of everyone I knew. Hell, in front of the entire town.

Glancing around, I met the expectant faces of the audience. My mother, Millie, tears glazing their eyes. My friends ready to root us on. Strangers anticipating only a positive ending to the romantic movie I was unwittingly acting out. I knew rejection of him would cause me more humiliation than I already felt.

"This was my mother's ring. Please. Will you marry me?" Xavier got my attention again, and I looked at the gigantic perfect diamond he was ready to place on my finger. Xavier's face appeared terrified, an expression I had never seen him wear.

I took a deep breath before giving my answer.

Chapter Fifteen

A PROPOSAL

"Yes."

The crowd erupted with cheers, and a large sigh of relief echoed throughout the tent. Xavier slid the ring on my finger and stood to embrace me tightly. He put his mouth over my ear and said, "I love you, Marissa. I know you're upset. I can explain later."

Glasses were being clinked in congratulations. Xavier pressed his lips to mine and tried to pry them open with his tongue slightly, but I wouldn't allow it. As he pulled back to look at my face, his expression had changed from terror to guilt or hurt. Good. He should be sorry.

Before I could run away and detonate the bomb ready to explode in my chest, my friends, mother, aunts, and some cousins rushed up to see the ring. Music was piped through the speakers, and waiters served the meal's first course from gold trays. Xavier held my hand,

and his buddies slapped him on the back, congratulating him.

"You poor, poor thing, Marissa. When he inevitably screws up, come on over to my place," Mason said. Xavier went to punch him in the arm, but Mason dodged at the last second.

"Way too young to get hitched, in my opinion," said Levi. As he said this, I noticed Elle glare at him, and he turned his face away from her to take a sip of his drink.

Sharice took the tension away and said, "Well, *I* think it's romantic." She had brought Maurice as her date. The two appeared comfortable with each other. All the other women agreed with Sharice. I noticed Kinsley was standing apart from Big G, who was loitering far away near the back of the group. Maybe that was done for.

We were called to sit at the head table as the first course awaited us. During dinner, Xavier tried to look at me several times, but I couldn't make eye contact with him. He tried to hold my hand, but I pulled away, hoping no one would see.

After eating, we posed for several pictures for the local newspaper, professional and amateur photographers snapping all kinds of angles of us all over the house. Millie or my mother would join them, trying to snap pictures with their phones. My friends got a few as well. I tried my best to pretend to be happily in love.

Before leaving for the night, my father pulled me aside and hugged me. He pressed his mouth onto my head and said, "If you want to back out, we will handle it. I want you to be happy, and you don't look happy." I nodded, holding back tears; I was trying to hide any emotions until it was safe to release them.

My mother and Millie hugged me, saying they couldn't wait to start on wedding plans. Mal embraced me, said welcome to the family again. He was so happy I was "doing this for us," mentioning "grandchildren" again. Xavier stood by my side with puppy dog eyes.

Xavier told me he would slow things down and wouldn't propose so soon. With James, I avoided confrontation and did anything to appease him. I had changed as a person. With Xavier, all I wanted at this moment was to provoke him.

Finally, finally, we made it back to his car. As he got in the driver's seat after helping me inside, he turned and said, "I know you're angry—"

"Xavier, I'm livid." I took off the beautiful ring and held it out. "Here. The show's over."

"What? No, no, no, no, please, Marissa, you will crush me. You'll end my life. Please don't give it back." He made some mewling groan, and I looked over. The man had genuine tears in his eyes; his face was shattered with emotion. "Please, wait. Please put it back on."

I sighed and put it back on for now. "Xavier, I told you it was too soon, and you went and did it anyway, *in front of everyone!* You know I hate being the center of attention, and you chose to do this in front of my entire family and friends... I am so angry with you. I want to break up."

"No, don't say that. You're not breaking up with me.

Please, will you let me explain? Can I explain some things to you?" I looked out the window. "I'm taking you to the cabin." He put the car in drive, and we headed out of town. I stayed silent, stewing in rage.

After arriving, I went to the kitchen to get a glass of water, trying to cool off. Xavier lit a fire in the fireplace, tossing his coat and tuxedo jacket on a chair. As he did, I explained, "Don't expect me to be here long. Make your speech, then take me home. And make it good, or we are done."

Xavier sat on the couch and pulled me by the hand to sit next to him. As he spoke, he put his head in his hands. "I loved my sister and mother; they were everything to me. My father was too busy with his business to care, but the three of us... we were a family. Yeah, my dad and I became close after, but when my mom and Olivia were alive, he avoided us."

He seemed perplexed but continued, "At first, I hated your whole family, but after watching you, I wondered if you had been hurt, too. Your mother doesn't have a clue. It's your father's fault. I don't know. I think I'm realizing maybe that's not true either." He was rambling.

"I'm confused," I said. "What does my father have to do with—?"

"Your uncle raped my sister. She died after... He murdered her."

My mouth dropped open.

Xavier said, "My sister was eleven at the time, the same age as you. My mother couldn't live with the grief.

173

She overdosed a few years after. I was a junior in high school. I found her."

Stunned, I sat silently for a moment. "Xavier… I don't know what to say. How did I not know this?"

"We kept everything out of the papers as much as we could. Pretty sure your father never mentioned anything. No one knew about my mother's cause of death."

"No, my father never talked about my uncle. We don't mention him. Ever. But you seem to think this was my father's fault?"

Xavier sighed heavily. "I wondered if he was an accessory if he knew what his brother did and kept it quiet. After my mother, I decided to look into him to see if I was right. I was going to gather some evidence and turn it over to the police, ruin your family as he had mine." He narrowed his eyes as he looked at me. "I saw you on campus and figured out who you were. It pissed me off to see you and your family living such happy lives while my family had been destroyed. I thought that if I had evidence, you'd do whatever I wanted to prevent me from going to the police.

"After I read your diary, I knew you had been a victim, too. But your dad, he didn't tell anyone what happened." Anger flashed on his face. "I just kept thinking if he had, my sister would be alive. My mother would be alive."

"But… my dad didn't know he would hurt other girls. How could he?"

"Yeah, he said that to me, too. He told me if he

could go back, he would have told the police. That he never guessed what your uncle was capable of."

"It was his brother. It must have been very confusing." I put my arm around Xavier's shoulders. "I can understand your anger. Xavier, I never knew about your sister. I swear."

"I know. My anger has been directed in the wrong place. It should have only been at the murderer." Xavier loosened his tuxedo bowtie. "I wanted to destroy you, but the longer I watched, the more... I didn't expect to fall in love with you. I tried to stop myself. These last two weeks, I tried to stay away like your father asked. I just couldn't."

He turned to me, grasped both my hands in his, and gazed into my eyes. "All Olivia wanted was to be someone's wife and mother. She played house all the time. She loved dogs and painting with watercolors. Marissa, my sister never got to live... Loving you from a distance for so long, I didn't want to waste another moment once you were in my arms. You got away from that monster; you escaped. You got to live. Instead of being so bitter about that, I wanted to give you everything she would never have once I fell for you. I wanted to give you a life."

Xavier had been trying to ruin my family and me but had fallen in love with me instead. I'd feel outraged and want revenge on someone if my family was destroyed. I recalled what he had told me about loving his family fiercely. He wanted to start a new family after his had been ripped from him. I leaned forward and placed my lips to his.

He looked into my eyes tenderly. "I'm so sorry, beautiful. I'm sorry I've rushed everything. Once I knew you were it for me, I couldn't wait for you to catch up. I just wanted to get started on life together. My life is nothing without you in it."

I wrapped my arms around him as he leaned forward, elbows on his knees. He looked broken.

"Please don't take the ring off. Please say you'll marry me even if it's not in the spring. We don't have to have a big wedding. I just want——" He stopped, looking around the firelit room. "I want all this with you."

I loved this man. I already could see myself in this house, with his children, living our lives. I had been putting an arbitrary timeline on when I thought we were *supposed* to do things, but he was right. Sometimes you just know, and I knew with him. I slipped my ringed hand into his. "Yes, Xavier. I'll marry you."

Xavier's face softened with relief, and tears filled our eyes. He grasped my face with both hands and pressed his lips to mine with our foreheads touching. "You just made my heart heal. I can feel it. You're saving me. I love you." He dipped his tongue in my mouth to deepen our kiss and gathered me to sit across his lap. His fingers threaded through my hair.

"I love you, too." I broke away to say.

"You'll be my wife?" he said in a whisper, checking to see my reaction.

I smiled into his lips. "Yes, I'll be your wife. And you'll be my husband."

Xavier growled and unzipped my dress, almost ripping it off when he caught a snag. I hurriedly unbuttoned his shirt and yanked on his cummerbund. He stood up while still holding me, then set me down in front of the fireplace. I stepped out of my dress while helping him unzip his pants and lower his boxer briefs. His heavy cock bobbed out, and I kissed the tip, glancing up at him.

"Fuck, kitten. I missed you," he said, throwing his head back for a second before meeting my eyes. I kneeled and began kissing the mushroom head of his reddened dick with my tongue, sucking the tip inside my mouth. "Stop. I have to taste you again."

I stood up, and he knelt in front of me, then lifted one of my legs over his shoulder. Xavier licked the seam of my lips with a wet tongue, then dove his entire face in. He poked fingers inside me and flattened his tongue on my clit. I humped his head while holding onto his hair.

"Hang on, I have an idea..." He stopped while I whimpered. I had been close to orgasm. Xavier lifted me by the waist and flipped me upside down so my face was in front of his full erection and my pussy was on his face. I was impressed with his physical prowess and began to devour his cock, taking it deep in my throat. Xavier moaned into my pussy as he pumped his tongue into my hole. His cock throbbed when I went in for a particularly deep dive and held myself down as long as I could before backing away for a breath. When I did, I heard Xavier say something into my tingling pussy, lightly tapping my clit with his teeth.

"I don't want to come in your throat. Fuck, I have to put my cum in your pussy." He flipped me back around and gently laid me on the nubby rug in front of the fireplace. His sweaty body slid up mine, his dick barely tapping at my entrance. He leaned on one elbow, grasping my face with his hand. We watched each other in ecstasy as he thrust into me, our bodies joining.

His hips scooped into me in slow motion, allowing me to feel every inch of him. He gazed into my eyes and said, "I love you."

I put my hand to his face. "I love you, too."

Speeding up his plunges, he leaned down to kiss me, his arms folding around my back, so we were tightly embraced. I wrapped my legs around his waist. "I'm serious, though. I can't wait to make you a mother. Fuck, it's all I think about when we're like this." He started slapping his hips to mine. "Just watching your belly get round with my baby… your tits getting swollen with milk…" I felt myself losing control. "I can't wait to breed my wife. You don't even need to think, just keep having my babies, and cook for me, kitten. Just be my little housewife. I'll take care of you. I'll take care of everything." My orgasm wrenched through me violently, and I screamed.

"Mmm, sounds like that's exactly what you want." Xavier was getting close as my body melted into the rug. "Ugh, I'll pump you so full of babies. You'll always have milk for me to snack on." As he was talking so dirty, I knew it was what my body wanted, too. I loved him taking over all control.

"Daddy, I want to have your babies." My palm still held his face, and as I said this, he groaned loudly.

"*Fuck…*" Xavier pulsed inside of me, filling my

pussy with so much of his cum, it spewed out when he started to pull back slightly. "I needed that. These last two weeks were torture without you." He bent down to kiss me deeply before saying, "Never again. I'm not letting you go."

We wrapped ourselves around each other and fell asleep in the warmth and glowing light of the fire.

Chapter Sixteen

CLOSURE

After the holiday party night, I felt closer to Xavier than ever. We never spent a moment apart. Now that it was winter break from school, we mainly stayed at our cabin or slept at his father's mansion if we wanted to hang out with friends in town the night before. My parents' house was too intimate for our loud romps not to be heard, so we never stayed there despite my mother's repeated offerings.

"Are you ready?" I slid my hand into Xavier's large, warm palm. He nodded in reply. "You don't have to do this. I wanted to see… to know. But if it bothers you—"

"No, I want to show you." Xavier put on a small smile for me. He pecked my cheek, pulled on his heavy black pea coat, and helped me with my trench coat.

Walking to the stable garage, he stopped in front of his row of vehicles, then chose the Land Rover. The forecast looked like snow, so the SUV was a wise choice. I pulled my scarf tighter around my neck and cap over my ears before climbing in the large leather passenger seat.

We'd stayed at the manor the night before to be closer to our errand the following day. Xavier didn't want his father to know where we were going. He said it was too difficult of a subject, and they didn't share much. Before he told me this, I had already invited Mal but didn't tell my fiancé. It would hopefully be a happy surprise.

As we pulled up to the cemetery, the skies dulled with thick gray clouds. The grounds were well-kept, and the asphalt of the lane was new. Several gravestones held beribboned wreaths left over from the holiday season. Snow began to drizzle from the sky when we approached a mausoleum near the back of the lot.

As I shifted in my seat, the crinkle of the cellophane surrounding the flower bundles in my lap cut through our silence. I cleared my throat. I prepared some comments I would make to help Xavier process things. Now, they all felt utterly ineffective. Like words could take away the pain of losing a mother and sister. How brash I had been!

Xavier parked the car just off the side of the drive. No other cars were around, so I supposed Malcolm had decided not to join us. I waited to mimic whatever Xavier wanted to do. He paused in the driver seat for what seemed to be several minutes, then jumped out. Not waiting for him to open my door, I got out, too.

Placing his arm around my shoulder, Xavier led me through a row of cement headstones. Before taking too many steps, however, a blue Jaguar pulled up behind the

Land Rover. Xavier stopped to watch as Malcolm and Millie got out of the car. Millie wore an all-white ensemble with a large, white, fuzzy hat. Malcolm carried a bouquet of white roses.

"Did you do this?" He peered at me suspiciously. I shrugged my shoulders. Xavier kissed my forehead. "I love you."

Mal sauntered quickly to Xavier and embraced him. Millie grabbed my gloved hand. Xavier and his father walked together, father's arm around his son, towards the gravesite.

Once we reached it, Mal squeezed his son's shoulder tighter. Millie and I stayed back until Xavier went for my hand to bring me closer to his side. Before attaching myself to Xavier, I laid my bouquets of lilies and snow-drops on the graves.

"Marissa, this was my mother, Lucia. She loved to laugh and loved the woods. Dad met her on a camping trip—"

Malcolm laughed. "She and her friends were *wild*. The four of my friends and the three of hers met up and decided to camp the rest of the weekend together. And that's all you'll ever know about all that."

"I think that's all I want to know." Xavier smiled shyly.

"I'm happy to meet you, Lucia. I wish we could have met sooner." Ugh. Everything I said sounded so wrong.

"And this was my sister, Olivia."

Malcolm let out a whimper and turned to Millie. He whispered, "Sorry, Xav. I can't." He had tears coming down his face. Millie smiled at me, then led Mal away to the cars.

Not knowing anything to say, I stood beside my boyfriend, holding his hand and not moving. We stood there a long while. The snow began to fall heavily around us. My mind kept thinking of things I wanted to say, but I kept quiet. Words seemed inadequate for the moment.

"Thank you." Xavier finally broke the silence. "I needed this." He kissed the top of my head, covered with my cap. "I'm ready." As we walked back to the vehicle, Xavier paused. "I want to do this again next year. For the same anniversary."

"Okay. Let's do it every year. Let's make it a *good* holiday. We'll bring our children, and they can get to know Olivia and your mother."

Xavier nodded and bit his lip before walking forward.

After our engagement, Xavier was more open with me. He admitted he used my Pinterest account to see what I liked and to explore my dreams; it's where he gathered the inspiration for our cabin. I had a board for my "dream house" and several for "future children," as well as my artistic inspirations. My stalker used them all to construct a blueprint of my deepest desires.

Like an unknown guardian angel, Xavier was in the background of my life for the past two years.

"What about that party where Trevor saved me from the roofie? Were you there?"

"Yeah, I was watching. Thought about interrupting to let you know what the game was." We were lying in

183

his bed at his father's mansion after a second round of "glad we're alive" sex.

"But you didn't," I said.

"No... back then I didn't care what happened to you. I was focused on trying to ruin your father's life. I thought you deserved to make your own choices. That was probably stupid of me," he said as he kissed my temple. "Mama C will be on us soon if we don't get downstairs for dinner."

After returning from the cemetery, Xavier was surprisingly (maybe not) horny. The man did have a voracious appetite for both food and sex.

"Wait, what about Mr. Hall... You said he would pay. Was—was the arrest all you?"

Xavier sighed and lay back, arm tucked around my body, holding me tight to his side. "I overheard you complain about that pervert for too long. I started to watch him with the other students, even took his intro photography class."

"You did?" I gazed into his eyes, rolling over on top of him.

"Kara and Brooke were in his class, too, and told me what his aim was—asking girls to his studio. Neither of them minded fucking him. They set up the camera for me. I had a computer program download the footage weekly but never checked it. Was just waiting for the right time, I think."

"And that day..."

"That day was definitely the right time. I was planning to murder him after I left you that night, but also wanted to be with you and couldn't do that in prison.

So, I started watching the feed instead and sent it to the police."

I stroked his hair back and gently let my lips brush his. He moaned and said, "Round three!"

We made love again while Mama C yelled from down the hall, "Get up, you lazy geese," and "Dinner is stone cold!"

Every afternoon, my mom and Millie would work on wedding plans. They were still shooting for a spring wedding. Evidently, that's when the Merrick country club was at its most beautiful. I just nodded and smiled and let them do their thing. The wedding didn't matter to me as much as my marriage.

I was getting used to the idea of becoming Mrs. Xavier Cardell. I would have preferred to elope or even have a small family gathering at the waterfall in the park, but Cardell Enterprises had many people to invite. Plus, with my friends and their dates and Xavier's friends and their dates... it was a lot of guests.

Even if we were moving fast, I knew Xavier was the one. I wanted to marry him and start our life together. His family welcomed me with open arms and treated me as if I was their daughter. My mother was just as obsessed with Xavier as I was. Xavier and my father had even started getting along. My dad made it to every Wednesday family dinner, and they had plans to play golf once the weather changed.

I imagined when we would get pregnant with our first child. Xavier talked about it often, especially before coming inside me. He was obsessed with planting his seed in my womb. I still had a year of college and thought it was probably best to wait until after graduation.

Instead of aspiring for some big career after university, I planned to spend my days working on my art, and our cabin was the perfect place to do so. Xavier had even made a studio on the bottom floor filled with natural light. I set up a portrait backdrop and practiced on him when he'd let me.

"You know, you're a much better cook than I am," I told him one evening when we were making dinner together at our house.

"Yeah, I am." He smirked and tasted the spaghetti sauce on the spoon as I gasped and hit him with the dish towel.

"You said you wanted me to be your housewife, but I think you should do the cooking."

He went to swat my ass with the spoon, but I dodged it. "How about we fuck for it?"

"What do you mean?"

"I mean, whoever comes first has to do the cooking." He put his arms around me and touched his nose to mine.

"That's stupid. We'd both suffer if I 'won.'"

He laughed. "You're right. How about if I cook, you clean up?"

"I am completely okay with that compromise."

Near the start of the spring semester, my mind flooded with ideas for my final project. The utter bliss I was living in being engaged to Xavier and planning our future together made me see fresh colors and new lights everywhere I looked. Everything became an inspiration. Everyone was a muse.

While reviewing my project notes in the campus coffee shop, I spotted a familiar face walking in next to an attractive man with deep chestnut hair. James noticed me in the corner and came over with a big smile.

"Hey, you! Long time no see!" I stood up to hug him in greeting. Genuine contentment filled my spirit.

"Yeah, it's been a while. How have you been?"

James sat down at my table. "It's been a bit crazy. I've missed you, though. Missed your friendship," he clarified.

"I missed you, too, James."

His tall companion approached with a couple of coffees, one for himself and one for James. James pointed to the chair next to him, and he sat. "Marissa, this is Neal... my boyfriend." He looked pleased for saying the title.

Neal smiled warmly at me and reached out his hand. "Oh, *you're* Marissa. James has said wonderful things about you. I'm so glad to meet you."

I greeted him and shook his hand.

Neal and James made an attractive couple. "So, how did you two meet?"

Neal chuckled. "It's a crazy story that involves tequila and the game Operation."

"And the tennis rackets," James added. They both laughed harder.

"Did your parents have their annual holiday party?" I asked James trepidatiously; I didn't want to offend Neal if he was not invited.

Neal snorted. "Oh, we went. His mother was about to have an aneurysm."

"Marissa knows all about my mother," James said.

"Yeah, she hated me. I bet she loved you," I said to Neal.

"No, his mother hates me. You're not alone there. I loved watching her head spin when we waltzed the first dance together," Neal said.

"That was because you stuck your tongue down my throat... not that I minded." James wrapped an arm around his boyfriend and kissed his cheek.

"Well, I'm going to be late for class. I'll see you around, Marissa. I hope you hang out with us some-time." He paused. "We could teach you drunken Opera-tion." James giggled across the table. He looked so happy.

I waved goodbye to Neal and turned to James. "He seems so nice, and, wow, is he hot."

James smiled. "Yeah, he is both." He looked down at the table, and I could tell he hesitated to bring up some-thing. "I heard you were engaged. I see the ring there... Xavier, huh?"

"Yeah. Listen, I'm sorry for the way things ended between us."

"Hey, it was my fault. As I said, I shouldn't have used

you. I should *never* have gotten with Jackson, that's for sure."

"What happened with Jackson?"

"He turned out to be a scheming snake. Plus, I never felt right using him to 'test out' my sexuality. He was the first guy I had a crush on, you know? He said he didn't care, but I did. Anyway, I am happy now and having a great time with Neal. I'm not putting sexual labels on everything anymore."

"I'm so happy for you, James. I'm glad you found him and seem... settled in who you are."

"I am, but listen. I'm glad I ran into you. The stuff about Jackson... Those TRZ guys are all conniving cunts." He grabbed my hands across the table. "Marissa, I don't want to see you get hurt. It is none of my business, but you can do so much better than him."

I pulled back on my hands. Xavier would murder him if he saw James touching me. "I appreciate your concern, but Xavier is pretty amazing. I love him."

He smiled sadly. "Like I said, none of my business. I care about you." He softly chuckled. "I guess I shouldn't expect an invite to the wedding."

I laughed. "I assure you I will be careful. Who knows, maybe after we are married, you two could also be friends."

"I highly doubt that." He got up to leave, and I hugged him goodbye. "Good luck." He kissed me on the cheek and left.

Chapter Seventeen

THE TRUTH

The winter was ending, and Theta Rho Zeta was planning their next quarterly Red Night event, aligning with Valentine's weekend. Xavier commanded that I remain next to him the entire night, shut up in his room with no guests allowed. I was fine with a night filled with sex with my fiancé, but I told him I planned to hang out with my friends, and he should as well. We'd been neglecting our groups by spending so much time alone together. Xavier was acclimating to compromise and noncommittally agreed. The promise of more anal helped.

I dressed in a tight black bandage dress and sky-high black strappy heels for the evening. Xavier loved my hair down so that he could pull on it, and I styled it the way I had for the first Red Night event. The girls and I rode to the party together, all ecstatic to know the president of TRZ's fiancé well enough to get personal invitations.

Red Night was well underway when we arrived late. Kinsley blamed me for taking too long. I scanned downstairs to find Xavier, but he was nowhere to be seen. I asked a few brothers if they had seen him, but no one had. There were only a few people in the hot tub, given the night's cold breeze, so I decided to head to his room—our room, to put my coat and purse in the closet.

As I approached the double doors, I heard moaning coming from inside. Xavier didn't want any guests up here, changing up the tradition, given his current relationship status with me. I wondered if people had sneaked in anyway. Xavier would be livid.

I opened the doors and saw Caitlyn rapidly riding a man on the sofa. All I could see was his dark head of hair. Trying to figure out what was happening, I stood in the doorway befuddled. Caitlyn looked me in the eyes and said, "Yes, Xavier, right there, daddy. You fuck me so good."

I gasped and felt my body turn to run away in horror. Or maybe I wanted to run to the sofa, rip her off my future husband, and murder them both. As I turned, however, I ran into a firm body. Xavier wrapped his arms around me, smiling.

"Hey, beautiful. They just told me you arrived." He leaned in to kiss me but stopped when he saw my stunned expression. "What's wrong?"

"I thought…" I turned my head back to his room, where Caitlyn was still grinding on the unknown man. Xavier followed my gaze and pushed me further into his room.

"What the *fuck*, Caitlyn. Get the fuck out of here."

"What? I was just having a little fun… like we used to." The guy she had been riding had dark hair, but it wasn't black like Xavier's. He quickly pushed Caitlyn off his lap, gave Xavier an apologetic look, then scurried off down the hall completely naked.

Xavier sighed. "No, you were trying to make it look like I was fucking you in here so my fiancé would get mad, or you'd try to make me jealous. Cut the bullshit. I know your games."

Caitlyn started to slide a negligee back on that had fallen to the floor. "Xavier, I know one woman isn't enough for you... The foursomes we'd have with Brooke, Kara, and me. I know you. Marrying her is a big mistake. Like I said, I'm up for the gig, and you can still have your cake and eat it, too. You wouldn't have to put up with a prude."

"As I have said many times before, I don't want you. Stop trying and leave me alone. You disgust me. Now, get the fuck out of my room. Your invitation here has been revoked." Xavier pulled out his phone to send a text.

Caitlyn started to cry and hurried from the room while Xavier turned to me and held me by the shoulders. "You think I would fuck someone else? You think I could ever cheat on you?"

"I thought... I didn't know what to think."

"Well, know that I can't even stand to look at someone else because they may think they'd have a shot with me. They don't. I'm obsessed with you. I love you, Marissa. You're mine, and I'm yours. There's no one else, and there never will be."

He shoved his lips to mine and wrapped his arms around my neck and waist. I could taste his cinnamon liquor as he stuck his tongue into my mouth to claim it. We began grinding on each other, him shoving his thick, hard cock into my belly, and I started to put one leg up around his waist.

A man in a bright yellow T-shirt knocked on the open door. "I'm so sorry to interrupt, Mr. Cardell. There's an incident at the front gate. A carload of men is trying to break in without invitations."

Xavier broke our kiss and sighed. While still gazing into my eyes, he said, "Tell them I'll be right there." To me, he said, "Do not move."

"Pfft, Xavier, I'm not going to stay up here all night. I'm going downstairs to hang with my friends if they aren't already fucking."

"You stick with Big G, then. Maybe Mason. Stay away from Levi, though." He thought for a moment. "Stay away from Mason, too. Just stick with Big G." He turned around, and I laughed as he walked with the guard downstairs.

I put my coat and purse in the closet and shut his doors before going downstairs. I saw Kinsley and Sharice near the dance floor in the large living room; Big G was standing with them, looking stoic. Elle must have been busy.

"Do you think they have any more of those little hot dogs," Kinsley asked with a slur as I approached.

"I can go check the kitchen. I know where they keep them. I gotta get myself a drink anyway." She handed me her cup, saying she needed a refill. Sharice shook her head behind her when she asked, indicating our friend had had too much.

"You're such a great friend. Come on, George, dance with me." She tried to drag her Viking of a boyfriend out onto the floor. He didn't budge.

As I headed to the kitchen, I saw Caitlyn with Jackson in the dining room. The two were in an animated conversation, and I tried to slip past them unseen.

"Oh... look who it is, Jack. The *fiancé*." Caitlyn laughed, obviously wasted now.

I tried to keep going, but Jackson stepped in front of me. I had to tilt my head to see him. "What do you want?"

"Wow, I can't believe you're drinking in your state."

"Uh... what state would that be, Jackson?"

"Pregnancy? With child? Bun in the oven?" He was snickering, and Caitlyn was laughing loudly behind him.

"You stupid bitch," Caitlyn mocked me. "You think he proposed and knocked you up because he *wanted* you?"

"What? I'm not pregnant."

Jackson sniggered, "You sure about that?"

I sighed. "Okay, what are you two talking about?"

Caitlyn narrowed her eyes with delight and, "Xavier doesn't inherit his trust fund unless he's married and has a baby by twenty-four, some stupid great-great-grandfather clause thing. Cardell Enterprises has been in trouble for years... He promised his daddy he would help with his inheritance once he got it." She chuckled without humor. "I offered, but he doesn't know a good thing when it gives him the best blowjob of his life. Besides, I wasn't stupid enough to get knocked up so young." She pointed at me up and down with her long black fingernail. "I guess some girls will do anything for a payout."

Was that true? Or was she being catty and making stuff up to mess with me? I knew Xavier was obsessed with getting me pregnant but was it all about his inheritance? Why did they assume I was pregnant?

Jackson pulled me aside with his big hand on my shoulder. He looked hurt or sad. "Word of advice, take a pregnancy test. Xavier switched out your birth control pills for blanks a while ago."

"What makes you think he did that?"

"I was the one to hand him the fakes. Last Red Night? Lose your bag? Yeah, he switched them then."

That didn't make any sense. I didn't think I was pregnant and continued to take my pills. Perhaps they were lying.

"Why are you telling me this, Jackson?"

Tears came to his eyes briefly. He said, "Because Xavier told me James was into me. Last Red Night, he told me to distract James, and we'd end up together. Said you were a lot more into him than James, and we'd both get ours." I was looking at a man with a broken heart. One that wanted revenge on my fiancé.

"James was into you, Jackson. More than me."

"Well, a lot of good that did. Caitlyn's a jealous bitch, and that's her motivation."

Caitlyn yelled, "Hey!" as he said this.

"I just want you to know what a conniving piece of shit your *fiancé* is." He looked at me with seriousness and said softly, "Take a pregnancy test, Marissa."

I dropped Kinsley's cup on the dining room table and turned to go upstairs. I wanted to check the pills in my purse I had in our room, Xavier's room. As I reached the stairs, Xavier came in the front door.

"Hey, beautiful." He saw the look on my face and turned to the left to see Jackson and Caitlyn. "What did they say to you?"

I ran up the stairs with Xavier close behind me. He was yelling at me to slow down and talk with him. When I reached his room, I frantically ran to the closet and opened my purse. I looked at my birth control pills, but they looked the same as always. Could fakes be this good?

"No, no, no, Marissa, listen, no. Listen to me." He was standing at the doorway like I might attack him.

"Is it true?" I asked again. "Xavier, is it true? Did you switch out my pills? D-did you only propose and try to impregnate me for an *inheritance*?" He stood still as a statue. "Oh. My. God. I am so stupid. It *is* true, isn't it?"

"Yes."

I wanted to run to the toilet to vomit; maybe I was pregnant. I darted to the door, but Xavier stopped me, putting his large body in front of the exit.

"But listen, I stopped. I switched them back. I couldn't do it."

"You better explain right now."

"My father, he's been on me about making my move on you for years, knowing the deadline... *fuck*. I didn't want to. I thought... ugh. I thought if I got you pregnant, you'd agree to marry me quickly; you'd be okay with it." He grabbed my shoulders to stop me from moving. He threw his head back and then looked at me. "Plus, fuck, Marissa, I want to put a baby in you so bad. It's an obsession." He pushed his hard body into mine. "I thought I could do it, switch out your pills, come inside you so many times you'd have my baby. I switched them out the first night I was with you."

I pushed on him. I wanted out of there. Wanted to get away from this person I no longer felt safe with. My trust in him was ruined.

"But I couldn't! I switched them back the next afternoon before I woke you up. I wanted you to *want* to get pregnant, to be bred by me. I wanted you to *want* to be my wife."

"I don't believe you. You are using me for *money*, Xavier! You switched out my pills, trying to secretly impregnate me! How could you? You're a monster!" I tried to shake off his arms.

"No! It was never about the money. I mean, yes, I could save my family's company; my father hasn't managed it well. It wasn't about me, though. It was about the legacy. My family. You. I wanted you and figured I could speed things along and help everyone."

"That's it, Xavier. We are done. I'm done with you. Let me go."

"No, please listen to me. I'll do anything. I'll give up the money. I don't even care anymore. Fuck the company. The only thing I care about is you. We don't have to get married until after the deadline… I'll prove it to you." He looked desperate. "But I'm marrying you. And you're having my babies… And you're not leaving."

I was hurt. I needed time to think about what had happened. He had done so many devious things that I wondered if anything good I believed about him was even true. Maybe my father, James, and Jackson were right. Xavier *was* manipulative and conniving, and I deserved better. I wanted a break to be alone, to sort out all the rush of thoughts and emotions I was having.

"Let me by."

"No. You're not leaving."

"Xavier, let me go. We can talk some other time, just not right now. I need to think. I want this to be over."

"No. We aren't ever over, I told you. And you're not leaving."

I pushed him. He braced his arms on either side of the closet doorframe. I slapped him. He slapped me. I held my hand to my face in shock.

"Now, you gonna be a good girl and be obedient, or do I need to lock you up?" he asked with fierce eyes.

"You're not locking me up. I'm so over this. I'm so over you." I tried to dip out under his arm, but he grabbed me and swung me over his shoulder. My short dress lifted, so my butt was exposed, pussy covered by a sliver of my black nylon thong.

"Guess you need to be locked up." Xavier wrestled my body as I tried to fight him, but heels and a tight dress didn't make for a good getaway outfit.

I fought against him as he got me down on the ground and held me there while he put on leather wrist restraints, my arms tied behind my back. A ball gag was shoved into my mouth and tied. He hauled me downstairs over his shoulder. I was terrified, not knowing where he was taking me or what his plans for me were. Every time I tried to scream for help, Xavier spanked me so hard that I would cry into the gag.

I heard cheers; guests of the party thought he was just enjoying Red Night with his woman. A few male voices spoke up as we walked downstairs.

"Cardell, you're so fucking crazy."

"Yo! Check out Cardell and his woman. They be into that kinky shit."

"Fuck her hard, Mr. President!"

We neared an area under the stairs where I heard Xavier open a door. He took us down a set of rickety steps to a stone basement. Through narrow dark passages, my body swayed as he lumbered to our destination.

The low-ceilinged room we entered smelled of mildew, and I could see through an opening in the far corner that there was a small bathroom with a dripping faucet. Xavier spun me around and tossed me on the bed. The silky red sheets were damp from the moisture in the air. I tried to push my legs to get away from him, but he pulled out ankle cuffs and strapped me to the metal footboard as I twisted in his grip. He did the same by unhooking my wrist restraints and moving my arms from around my back to up over my head, securing them to the headboard. I could move my body some-what, but not by much.

Now that I could see, the room had a strange, small A-frame bench and a wooden chest with a padlock attached. A large red velvet rug covered the floor. There were hooks on the ceiling.

Xavier stood at the end of the bed and crossed one arm over his chest; the other he leaned against his chin. "I tried to spoil you. I tried to give you everything you could ever want, Marissa." He began to pace at the end of the bed. "Apparently, that wasn't good enough. You wanted to leave because you thought I was a monster…" He stopped his pace and dropped his arms.

His icy-blue eyes glowered at me. "That was me being nice. Now, you're going to meet the monster."

Xavier turned on his heel and left.

Chapter Eighteen

RULES

I was trapped, tied to a bed with a ball gag in my mouth. I couldn't scream; I tried until I was hoarse. I couldn't move, and I hurt all over. I had to pee for hours and would have to all over myself if no one came soon. I had no idea what time it was; the sconces on the walls barely gave the room enough light as it was. Xavier had been gone a long time, and I didn't know when, or worse if, he was coming back. As I had always feared, the monster had locked me up in a dark basement.

I must have dozed off when I heard shuffling outside the wooden door. I opened my eyes and could just turn my head enough to look. Xavier walked in with a pile of towels, and I felt relief and terror simultaneously. I tried to moan or whimper but couldn't.

"Aw, kitten, look at you so eager to see your master." He closed the door. The lock was on the outside of the door. I had made that out earlier, looking around the room, trying to plan an escape. He went into the attached bathroom and ditched his items.

When he returned, he stood at the end of the bed for a while before speaking. "Here are the rules. You only speak when I ask you something, and then I expect to be addressed as master or sir. Nod your head if you understand." I nodded, and he undid one ankle strap—the relief of being able to move flooded my body until tears came to my eyes.

"You will not attempt to escape. If I find that you attempted to escape, you will be punished. Nod if you understand." I nodded, and he released the second ankle. I curled my legs up to my chest.

"You are to greet me at this door on your knees, hands behind your back. Nod if you understand." I nodded. He released a wrist strap while carefully monitoring if I would try to hurt him or run away. I was so weak, I couldn't. He had the upper hand here.

"You will swallow my cum whenever I choose to give it and will eat it first before you earn any meal. Nod if you understand."

I was already so hungry. Now he was telling me I couldn't eat unless I sucked him off. Was he crazy? Yes. Yes, he was.

He smacked my face. "I am done giving orders twice. Perhaps I should leave these on."

I nodded emphatically that I understood him. He seemed to consider a moment, then released my last restraint. I got into the fetal position. It felt so good to move, and my body surrendered to the comfort. I just wanted to go to the bathroom.

"You will not masturbate or orgasm unless I deem it. Nod if you understand." I nodded, and he undid my gag. Oh, the pleasure of closing my mouth and moving my jaw. Things I always took for granted.

"You have permission to go to the toilet. Clean yourself up and get naked. I'm going to give you your first meal of the day."

I almost fell, given how stiff my joints were, but made it into the bathroom, which had a rickety old door that scraped the stone floor as I tried to shut it. There was one hanging bulb, a nasty toilet, and a rusted sink basin. A small broken and hazy mirror sat above the drippy faucet. Xavier had laid a bar of soap, washcloths, a toothbrush, toothpaste, and a body towel on the toilet. At least he hadn't deprived me of those.

I considered breaking the pipes so someone may rescue me, or I could use it as a weapon. Maybe I could use the glass from the mirror to stab him. If I hid in the corner, perhaps he would leave me alone. I knew none of those plans would work, at least not now when I felt like I may faint. I did not want to displease him and get punished, so I hurried to take care of myself in the bathroom and undressed.

When I returned to the room, Xavier stopped me with his powerful voice. "Drop to your knees and crawl to your master." He stood next to the bed.

I did as he said. When I approached, he ordered, "Sit back on your heels and place your hands behind your back. Don't look at me. I'm too angry with you still and may not feed you."

Xavier was angry with *me*? What had I done? He

was the one who lied and tried to replace my birth control pills! My cheeks flushed with anger. Suddenly, my backside burned. I realized Xavier whipped me with a leather flogger hidden behind his back.

"I won't give a command twice. I will leave you here without food unless you obey me promptly. I also expect you to respond to my commands. Now, sit back on your heels and put your hands behind your back."

I sat, put my hands behind my back, and said, "Yes, master."

Xavier came over to me and unzipped, taking out his semi-erect large cock. "Get me hard. If you bite, you will be punished. You don't eat unless I feed you." I reached to grab his penis, but he smacked my hands. "Hands behind your back." I put them back.

He moved closer, and I used my tongue to pull him inside my mouth. Then, he grabbed my head and began to fuck it. Once again, he would shove to the back of my mouth and pinch my nose, closing off my air. This time, I was more used to the sensation and could tell myself to relax and allow him to determine when I needed to breathe.

Xavier must have felt it when I relaxed and said, "Yes, I control your breathing. I control your eating. I control when you move and how. I control everything about you."

My knees were sore, my arms hurt, and my neck was strained. I was choking and gagging, spitting up whenever he would pull out. He had taken pleasure in me the night at Manny's, but now he seemed angry, distant. I was being used.

This wasn't about connection. This was about control.

I felt his cock start to pulse deep in my throat with one hard shove. As he neared climax, he said, "You will learn to love my cum above all food. It is necessary for your life. You will crave it above anything else. You'll be begging for this meal I gift to you." He shoved in and almost came but stopped. "Eat and thank me for it."

Ropes of hot cum spurted straight down my throat so I couldn't taste him. As it hit my stomach, I felt queasy after not having anything to eat for who knows how long. He didn't even groan with pleasure as he normally did; he just emptied himself into my stomach and pulled out. I felt cold, dejected.

"Get down on all fours. Do not move." Xavier zipped himself up, and I lowered my head to the ground. I heard him go out the door before coming back in. After some shuffling, I could see him setting up a small folding table and placing a tray of food on it. The smell made me ravenous.

"Here is your food, but remember it does not provide you the nourishment you need like your master's cum." I started to rise when he said, "You may rise and eat the food I have gifted you."

He turned and left, locking the door when he had shut it. I quickly rose and saw a paper plate filled with scrambled eggs, bacon, and toast. There were plastic cups of orange juice and water. There was no fork to eat with. I didn't care. I folded the plate in half and shoveled the eggs in, swallowing them whole. Once it hit my belly, I slowed down to enjoy the bacon and toast. After eating and feeling sated, I realized I should have kept some for later in case my captor didn't return.

I didn't know what to do with myself. After walking around the room, inspecting every inch, I tried to see if there was any way to escape. The door was impenetrable. Other than the broken mirror in the bathroom, I couldn't see any way to form a weapon. The pipes on the sink wouldn't budge. There was no lid to the toilet— it was one of those that sat into the wall. The pipes were so rusted that it was impossible for me to take them apart.

The chest with the padlock offered no solutions. Items rattled within when I tried to move it. The hooks in the ceiling wouldn't budge when I stood on the bed to try to unscrew them from the beams overhead. I must have spent hours looking at every item, then placing them back so Xavier wouldn't know. I feared his punishment.

I brushed my teeth. I drank water from the sink. I washed my face. I tried stretching. Finally, I grew so bored that I decided to sleep my imprisonment away.

I awoke with my thumb being forced onto a cold, hard surface. Xavier held my phone in his hand and unlocked it while I was asleep. I started to move, but he commanded, "Don't move." He was typing away on the phone as if texting someone. The dejected feeling came back as I realized he had barely looked at me since he threw me in the room. I couldn't stand it, not having his blue eyes on me.

My body wanted to push him and rush out the door, knowing it was unlocked while he was inside. I must have jolted a bit, but he moved with the speed of a cheetah and grabbed my arms, twisting them behind me while dropping my phone on the bed. He finally looked at me, his face filled with rage. "I said: Do. Not. Move."

My arms were forced into the wrist restraints attached to the headboard. I whimpered at the roughness of his touch. "Why are you so angry with me? I'm the one angry with you. Shouldn't we talk about this?"

"Rule number one. What is it?"

I sighed. I just wanted to have a conversation. I was done playing this game. "Not to talk to you unless you ask me a question… sir."

"You broke that rule. You will be punished." He unhooked the wrist restraints from the headboard and locked my wrists behind my back.

"Get up and take position on the breeding bench."

Breeding bench? Was that what that weird thing was? Was he still trying to *breed* me? I walked over to the bench and straddled it, placing my knees on the pads indicated. Xavier locked my ankles to it. He unhooked my arms before restraining them on the other pads. I was on all fours, supported by the bench. From this position, my pussy and ass were completely exposed and at the perfect height for him.

He went to the chest and unlocked it. He gathered something from inside. As he approached me from behind, he said, "Ass, mouth, or pussy. I will give you a choice as I am such a benevolent god."

Tied to a breeding bench, all my holes were at his disposal, and I had no way of controlling my movements, or at least not by much. I hadn't taken a birth control pill since the night of the party before I left to come to the manor on Red Night. That meant I had likely missed one or was about to unless Xavier brought them for me.

"Are you… are you going to give me my birth control pills?" Pain immediately spread across my ass as Xavier caned it. I screamed.

"I asked you a simple question. You are to answer it with respect. Ass, pussy, or mouth."

"I can't make that decision, sir, unless I know… Please."

He caned me again, and I cried.

"Ass… I'll take ass." He caned me again. "Master, please."

"Please, what?"

"Fuck me in the ass, master, please."

"It sounds as if you think you'll enjoy it. You won't." He took the ball gag and shoved it in my mouth. I felt lube drizzle all over my ass and his finger plunge repeatedly in and out. Each time I released an involuntary moan, he would cane me, and I would scream in pain.

He shoved his cock deep into my ass with a forceful thrust. He was right. With how rough he was being, I wasn't enjoying it. Not like before. I chose my ass because I was afraid he wouldn't give me my pills and would end up impregnating me on the bench.

I hoped he would finish soon and return to being my Xavier. Worse than the pain in my ass was the pain of missing my lover: his tenderness, his warmth, and caring nature. His laughter. I cried into the gag as he came inside me forcefully. He barely grunted as he did so before quickly sliding out.

"I should leave you like this. You have been quite disobedient." I heard him zip up and rummage in the chest, locking the padlock. He went out the door, and I was afraid he would leave me there, but he came back, and I immediately caught the scent of savory foods. He placed another tray on the table and took the old one away. He then came over and unbound me, releasing me from the gag. I remained still, cum dripping out of my ass.

"You may get up and eat." I arose, and he walked out the door.

Before he left, I sobbed, "Xavier, please. Please, how long are you going to keep me here?"

He was holding the door open, getting ready to step through. His back to me, he turned his head slightly to say, "Until you want to stay." Then, he left and locked the door behind him.

Chapter Nineteen

LIFE UNDERGROUND

Life underground was settling into a routine. Xavier would come in, probably in the mornings, feed me his cum, then serve me breakfast. Likely in the evenings, after his classes, he would present again. He would tie me to the bench and ask, "Ass, pussy, or mouth." I would get a second meal after that deposit.

I would scramble to the door and hurriedly kneel, hands behind my back, whenever I would hear him start to open the door. I didn't know how long I had been in the basement and was worried about my family not knowing where I was and about missing my classes. Xavier had not given me birth control pills, and I wasn't going to ask again. I didn't like the cane, and he knew it.

I always chose ass during the evening visits because my throat was sore from the morning's meal, and I was afraid of getting pregnant by choosing pussy. Each fucking on the bench became progressively more difficult. I started to enjoy getting taken roughly in the ass, my clit rubbing against the end of the bench. The problem was, anytime I experienced some pleasure, he would cane me and remind me I was not allowed to come. When I developed a thirst for the morning's meal and tried to back him out of my throat to taste him, my face was met with a slap.

Whenever shuffles of steps on the stones indicated Xavier's approach, I would get hot and bothered. Even sitting at the door waiting for him in my position made me wet between my thighs. When I would get into bed to sleep the days or nights or afternoons away, I would remember how his cock felt roughly taking my ass and started to put fingers on my clit, but I would stop myself for fear he was watching me through a hidden camera.

The time alone left me with nothing to do but think and fantasize. I imagined art projects, photographs, oils, and watercolors I wanted to create if I ever escaped. I imagined what my little studio at the cabin would look like with the lighting setup I had in mind. I couldn't see myself anywhere else, but in that refuge of peace with the Xavier I knew before. I became desperate for it. Clinging to the image of us, there together... it was my solace.

I missed him. I missed us. After crying over missing what we had, I realized I had almost walked away from it all. His words came back to me about not caring about the money and getting married after his inheritance deadline to prove how much he wanted me. He would let his legacy go for me. His family's business would be destroyed because I didn't trust that he truly wanted to marry me.

I remembered the day he first took me to our house and told me all the things he admired about me, what he saw that was special. The feeling of love that showered me when he showed me my portraits in the art gallery. Xavier took care of me and eradicated my enemies. He protected me. He did try to give me everything I wanted; he spoiled me.

I hadn't trusted him, thinking he was cheating on me and accused him of tricking me when all he had done was love me. I didn't even give him time for an explanation. I just wanted to leave. I was giving up so easily on something that was supposed to last a lifetime.

I understood his rage.

However, he wasn't allowing me to talk to him. I didn't know how to tell him all this. I wanted to beg his forgiveness for trying to abandon him like his mother and sister. Beg his forgiveness for thinking he would ever cheat on me and that I would never leave or walk away from us when I became angry with him or if we argued —that I was in this for life. That I wanted to get married and have his children.

And what was the holdup? Why couldn't I help his family, soon to be Xavier's own business, and our own child's legacy by getting married and pregnant now? If I loved this man, and I did, why wouldn't I want to help him and his family by speeding up the timeline of when things were *supposed* to happen?

How was I supposed to tell him this without using my words?

I could communicate with him by being the best slave he could have. I would be obedient and compliant, which I knew pleased him. After all the times wondering what my own desires were, I realized that submitting to him brought me the most pleasure. This evening, when he asked me which hole, I knew what my answer would be.

Shuffling off the bed, I dropped to my knees and put my hands behind my back, staring at the floor. I didn't know what time it was, but I wanted to wait for him. The longer I waited, the more I drenched my thighs with my wetness. Finally, the sound of the familiar shuffles met my ears.

Xavier opened the door and closed it slowly. He stood in front of me, and I could see his leather shoes in my field of vision. I had the overwhelming desire to reach out and lick his shoe, to just be able to touch him in any way. I believed he could sense this and moved closer. I didn't dare to look up.

"I smell your arousal. I can smell your pussy. Has my kitten missed me?" My heart raced at his pet name for me. This was working. "Lick my shoe."

I bent down quickly at the order to lick his shoe greedily with my tongue as he chuckled. "Hmm, I see I have broken you. Good girl."

He moved close enough that I could not lick him again. I sat back, head down. "Look up at me, slave." As I looked at him with deference, with love, he seemed to consider my face, maybe noticing a change there. He reached under my jaw to hold it and stroked my cheek with his thumb. His expression remained cold and detached, however. I closed my eyes to remember the feel of his gentle touch for later.

"Are you ready for your first meal?"

"Yes, master," I said, but not too eagerly. I didn't want him to know how much I was looking forward to it. He moved his hand to the back of my head and put his cock inside my mouth and fucked me. This time, however, I didn't struggle whenever he cut off my air. I became the best hole for him to fuck. I savored every moment of it, craving his cum. I needed it. I couldn't live without having it inside me all the time. Whenever he would pull back, I could take it out of my mouth and rub my face all over his dick. He stroked my face when I did so.

"That's it, kitten. Worship your god, my cock. Mmm, I can tell your cravings have set in." He pushed it in again and pumped harshly, attempting to see if I would gag, pull away, or choke. I let him do whatever he wanted and enjoyed hearing his groans and moans of approval. He pulled his cock back to my tongue and said, "You deserve this reward. I will grant you your craving." He came all over my tongue and pulled out more. Some landed on my mouth and cheek.

I scooped all the cum onto my finger and slid it into my mouth. I savored every bit of it before swallowing as slowly as I could. I felt whole again for a moment with his cum inside of me. I knew it wouldn't last long, though, and I would need it again soon. I lowered my face to the floor in reverence.

Xavier raised my face with his hand and stroked my cheek again. He then patted my hair and said, "You're such a good pet, kitten." He went to get my food tray, but I was full of his cum in my belly. I didn't need anything else as long as I had his nourishment.

After he set the tray down, he turned to me. "I think you're starting to want to stay." I did. He was right.

The hours passed. I had eaten the food he left for some energy. I cleaned myself and made myself as presentable as possible. As I napped, I started to design a nursery in our cabin. I imagined what our baby would look like. I fantasized about our future days on the lake, cooking dinner together if he would teach me, getting into arguments about stupid things, and having makeup sex in the hot tub.

As I sensed my master's approach, I got into position and waited. Once again, I flushed with juices between my thighs the longer I sat. It almost felt more natural to wait in this position than any other by now.

My master opened the door and chuckled as he saw me sitting back on my heels, waiting in the correct position and not having to scramble like other times. "Kitten must miss her owner. She's being such a good kitty today." He sniffed the air again. "And, you're soaking the air with your scent. Take your place on the breeding bench."

I did as instructed. He seemed to assume I would answer "ass" again and got out the lube. "Ass, pussy, or mouth."

"Pussy, master."

He didn't speak. Master waited so long to move that I almost broke position to try and look over and see if he were still there.

"Ass, pussy, or mouth?"

"Pussy, master. Please fuck my pussy."

He again did not move. I heard the lube bottle shut. Suddenly, he knelt beside me so I could see his face, and it was my Xavier. The cold, harsh master was not there. He brushed a piece of my hair out of my face. "Marissa, I was angry. I haven't given you your birth control. Are you sure?"

"Yes, please, master. Fuck my pussy. Breed me, master."

Tears came to his eyes, and at that sight, I began to tear up as well. He quickly undid my wrist and ankle restraints and held me against his body. I began to sob and shake uncontrollably in his embrace. His hands were in my hair, around my waist, clutching me tightly. He moved to kiss me passionately, but it was so sloppy that we bumped noses and almost bit each other's lips off. He licked up the tears falling from my face.

"I love you, Marissa. I love you. I'm sorry. I should have told you about the inheritance. We don't have to do this; I just have to have you—"

I interrupted him before he could continue, "I love you, Xavier. I *want* to get married. Now. I *want* to have your baby. Now. I'm so sorry I didn't trust you. You have given me everything. You have given me life… a life I have dreamed of having and one I can only have with you. I'll never threaten to leave again. I'm here. I'm not going anywhere. I'm yours. I'm yours, Xavier."

His eyes were glistening when I looked into them. He kissed me desperately and took me to the bed. He laid me back and spread my legs. His lips went to my pussy lips, and he ate me like a starving man. The thick middle finger he put inside me was enough for me to hump, then come all over his face while screaming. I had such pent-up lust I couldn't stop, and when he continued to lick and suck on my clit, tiny circles, and pulses added randomly, I came again.

"Xavier, please. I mean it. Please fuck my pussy. I'm ready."

He laughed into my cunt. "Kitten, I want to. I just don't want to do it in this fucking dungeon." He sat me up as I was panting from the last orgasm. He slipped my body onto him as he sat down, so I sat sideways on his lap. I put my head into his neck, and he stroked my hair.

"I'm going to take you home. I'm going to pamper you. And then I'm going to put a baby inside of you. Would you like that?"

I nodded and said, "Yes, very much. I love you."

"I love you, too." He kissed my forehead.

He found my dress from the party and brought it to me to put on. Then, he held my hand as we alighted the rickety stairs from the basement. He told me to wait in the entry while he grabbed my coat and purse.

On our way to the house, I relaxed in his Land Rover with the heat blazing on me, warming me all over. Before we left, Xavier handed me a blanket, a bag of popcorn, and a bottle of water. As he drove, he kept his hand on my thigh and kept glancing over at me as if I had been lost and he had just found me.

"How long has it been?" I asked him in a daze.

"Six days. It's Friday night."

"Oh. Does—" I started to ask.

"Your family and friends think you've been sick with

the flu. They knew you were with me. I told the school you were sick and got your assignments. I had my personal, well, *our* doctor write you an excuse for the missed lectures. I paid a brother in your class to write your paper for you... it's pretty good if you want to use it."

He had thought of everything.

"What were you going to do if I was down there another week? A month?"

"I couldn't stand it, Marissa. I was going to let you out tomorrow and try something else. The distance... It was driving me mad." He paused. "When I saw your eyes this morning, I thought maybe there was a chance we could talk things out. That you'd hear me out and be with me."

"I should have listened to you instead of trying to run away, not trusting you. I know you love me, and the money means nothing to you. I understand you want to help your family. They'll be my family, too. Our children's legacy... We were going to get married and have kids, anyway, may as well do it and help Cardell Enterprises while we're at it."

Xavier grabbed my hand, lifted it to his mouth, and kissed it. "Seriously, I will give it up for you. We can wait; I'll wait for you forever. But you've got about twenty minutes to change your mind, beautiful. Otherwise, I'm blowing up that cunt with my sperm."

"Oh, what a thing to tell the grandchildren..." I laughed.

Arriving at the cabin, Xavier carried me across the threshold and straight to the hot tub. We dropped our clothes and got in. He sat behind me, massaging me all over, kissing my neck, ears, and back, rubbing his fingers through my hair and on my scalp. I was putty in his crafty hands.

I turned around in his lap and wrapped my legs around his waist, arms around his neck. He stood up, holding me by my butt cheeks, and slid inside my pussy. Our eyes locked onto each other as he pounded up into me. Neither of us would last long. I threw my head back with the pleasure he was giving me with each slap of his hips. "Look at me, love. I'm going to breed you. I'm going to put my baby inside you now. You still want that?"

"Yes, Xavier, please, please." I panted.

"I need you to come with me… come with me and push this cum into your womb. You ready? Come with me, beautiful." His face crinkled with mine as we both groaned and yelled in sync. I felt his waves of hot cum enter my pussy, filling me completely.

We began to kiss each other, sucking the breath from one another. He stayed inside me as long as possible before he sat down with me still in his lap.

"Give me ten. Then we're going again… and again… and again…"

I laughed and nodded in reply. It was going to be a long night.

Epilogue

It was raining. This was typical for early April, but I was worried it would mean we'd lose our first location for the ceremony. It was the only thing at our wedding I'd asked for. As I stood in front of the full-length mirror, I gazed out the window in my old bedroom at my parents' house and twisted my fingers.

"It's still going to be beautiful. Besides, rain on your wedding day is good luck," said Sharice.

She, Kinsley, and Elle were helping me get dressed, then heading to the ceremony site. My mother was making final plans with Millie downstairs.

"I know, I was just hoping... I just wanted it to be at my spot."

My father knocked, and I told him to come in. He gasped when he saw me in my custom couture gown. It was made of ivory silk. Off-the-shoulder straps hung from a tightly fitted bodice showcasing a sweetheart neckline and crafted from hand-embroidered floral appliqués. The trumpet shape landed in a soft cathedral train of tulle. The color made my skin glow, and the form accentuated every curve of my body. I loved it.

Unfortunately, the tailor had to let out the bodice slightly before the big day. Even though I was only a few weeks pregnant, I had gained some weight already. Not enough for anyone to notice, but the dress wasn't very forgiving. It was good we were going ahead with the wedding before I couldn't wear the beautiful gown at all.

I had been worried that our baby wouldn't be born in time to meet the requirements of Xavier's trust. His family's lawyers assured us, however, if I was still pregnant, the language was not specific enough to preclude him from receiving the full amount.

I was relieved we could help Cardell Enterprises. Xavier had great ideas on how to make it profitable again. Perhaps someday, our child would take it over if they wanted. We decided our child would have the choice of running the company or not.

My mom burst through the door behind my father, who had advanced and tried to hug me without touching me. "Look! Outside! We're going to the park!"

I glanced outside, and sure enough, the rain slowed to a drizzle while the sunshine peeked through. The clouds were rolling away. I couldn't cry, not yet.

"They're drying off the chairs and setting everything up now. You ready?" Mom asked.

The only thing I requested was a small ceremony of family and close friends at my favorite place, the waterfall in the state park. I had shown Xavier where I wanted to exchange our vows, and we made love on a nearby rock before he said, "Yeah... this is the place."

The reception was the event of the spring. The entire town was invited to the Merrick country club after our ceremony. It wasn't my ideal, but Xavier said to keep my eyes on him, and we'd push through. Then, we could head to our honeymoon in Bali.

I rubbed my stomach instinctively, cradling the life inside me. I couldn't wait to meet our baby. Xavier was the happiest I had ever seen him when I took the fourth pregnancy test, showing him the positives. We held each other, forehead to forehead. I cried tears of joy. Now I couldn't wait to see his face as I walked through the trees to meet him as my husband for the first time.

Once we arrived at the ceremony site, I peeked at the decorations, trying not to be seen. The natural wooded trail had been covered with white rose petals to make an aisle. Rustic benches were brought in for the few guests in attendance. Through the trees and around a bend in the path, I could make out the love of my life standing in front of the water.

I stood next to my father. He was just as nervous as I was. He looked at me and said, "Remember when I said he wasn't good enough for you?"

"Yes, Dad."

"He's still not, but there's no one better. I am so happy for you two and love you both." He kissed my cheek, and I could see tears in his eyes. "And can't wait to meet our grandchild."

I willed myself not to cry. "Thanks, Dad. I love you, too."

The musicians (including Sharice) struck up their chords, and we proceeded to the aisle. As I rounded the corner tree, Xavier and I locked eyes. His hand went over his mouth in shock, and he immediately teared up, which made me finally release the tears I had been holding back. There went my will. I reached into my bouquet to get my handkerchief and dotted my eyes as we passed our close friends and family.

I listened to the words of our vows carefully as Xavier spoke them to me and repeated mine with sincerity. The intimacy of our first kiss as husband and wife nearly took my breath away, and we probably would have kept going, except I heard Levi say, "Dude! You're gonna get her pregnant." Everyone nearby that heard him laughed. We hadn't told our friends about the baby yet, so Xavier and I stopped kissing long enough to give each other knowing looks before heading back up the aisle together, hand in hand, as husband and wife.

"It's here, beautiful!"

We'd been married five years. My feet hurt as I stood in my studio adjusting the lights, trying to snap a portrait of a cranky toddler. The third trimester of pregnancy was annoying, and I couldn't wait for nap time, mine and my daughter's.

"Come on, Olivia." I gathered up my daughter, who was crying because I made her sit on the stool "like a big girl" for her portrait when all she wanted was to spin in her princess dress. I picked her up and made my way to the stairs when my husband ran down to meet us.

"Stop, put her down. Kitten, you can't carry this ragamuffin while pregnant." Olivia grabbed him around his neck. "Someone looks sleepy anyway. Nap time." He handed me an envelope as he started to sway with Olivia in his arms.

I ripped it open. "You are cordially invited to The Olivia Cardell Watercolor Studio Grand Opening," I read out loud. "It's happening!"

Cardell Enterprises had turned a corner. With the new profits Xavier had earned with his business acumen, we were using most of the money to give back to the community. In honor of his sister, he had envisioned a place where children of those less fortunate could come after school and learn art in all forms. We found volunteer tutors in writing, painting, sculpting, photography (like me), and even ceramics. Now our dream had become a reality.

Along with Sharice, we eventually planned to add a music portion to the studio. Who knew how much we could expand after that? The place had taken up most of my time over the last three years of development, and I felt pure joy at the sense of accomplishment holding the invitation in my hand.

"Mommy!" Ryan, our firstborn, ran down the stairs and tried to skip the last three.

"Ryan, careful. Don't do that," I said firmly.

"Can I go to the lake today?"

"Ask your father. Olivia and I are taking a nap."

I took Olivia back from Xavier, who briefly kissed me on the lips, then said to our son, "Yeah, let's go. I can finish up work later." Xavier often worked from home to be near us. Said he couldn't stand to work in his stuffy office in town.

"Hey," Xavier got my attention. "I'll um… see you in a bit? Like an hour?" He cleared his throat.

I kissed him and smiled slyly. "Yes, Mr. Cardell. I'll be waking up from my nap and will need your help in the bedroom…"

As I put Olivia down for her nap, I peered out of the window where I could see Xavier teaching Ryan how to dive from the dock. Ryan had no fear, and I could tell Xavier kept telling him to be careful. I rubbed my belly. Maybe it was the pregnancy hormones, but I teared up at the vision of my daughter sleeping softly in her little princess bed, my son running and jumping wildly from our dock, laughing each time my husband scolded him for not minding.

Because of the choices I had made, I was now living my dream life with the love of my life.

Acknowledgments

To my friends and beta readers, my utmost gratitude. To the ARC readers and followers on social media, you are amazing! Thank you for supporting a new author though I know how long your TBRs are!

Thank you especially to my partner in this process, Jen. You have been a true friend and aid in my darkest hours. To Dr. K, who wanted our hero to glitter, but I said no. Thank you for reading, even though this is not your genre; you read only because you're amazing.

To my husband, who wants all my writings to be made into a movie, thank you for being there to answer weird questions about penises in the middle of the night. You were my editor, my partner, and my inspiration for too many of my favorite quotes in this book (and, no, dear readers, you can't know which ones).

About the Author

Kitty King is a romance writer by day and a psychiatrist by night. Kitty enjoys reading erotic romance tales just as much as writing them. Besides reading and writing, she spends her spare time hiking with her husband and playing with her overzealous dogs.

http://authorkittyking.com

amazon.com/author/kittykingauthor

instagram.com/kittykingauthor

tiktok.com/@kittykingauthor

Also by Kitty King

THE COLOR SERIES

Red Night: Xavier's Delight (Book 1)

Blue Film (Book 2)

White Hole (Book 3)

STANDALONE

The Wrong Man

Full list on her website:

http://authorkittyking.com

Next in the Series...

Curious about what was going on with Elle & Levi?

Want to see *Red Night* events from different perspectives?

Read *Blue Film*, the second book in The Color Series!

Drunk at an all-inclusive and pretending to be an engaged couple... what could go wrong?

Elle

Ever since we were little I had a crush on Levi. The happiest day of my childhood was our pretend wedding at recess. Then, he turned into my biggest bully. Ending up at an all-inclusive resort together, intoxicated on the island's breezes and fruity drinks may lead to a bad decision... like walking down the aisle again.

Levi

I don't do relationships. But I have always wanted Elle, ever since our fake wedding in elementary school. It's why I was so mean to her. Now we are drunk and alone on an island. She looks too good to resist. Maybe I could make an exception for her.

Old flings, new whims, borrowed rings... *blue film.*

• An X-rated romantic comedy

• Childhood bully-to-lovers story

• Dual POV

Printed in Great Britain
by Amazon